Alfred Tennyson, S. N. Cook

The Wanderers Return

A drama, in four acts, founded on Tennysons poem of

Alfred Tennyson, S. N. Cook

The Wanderers Return
A drama, in four acts, founded on Tennysons poem of

ISBN/EAN: 9783337343743

Printed in Europe, USA, Canada, Australia, Japan

Cover: Foto ©Andreas Hilbeck / pixelio.de

More available books at **www.hansebooks.com**

THE WANDERER'S RETURN.

A DRAMA,

In four Acts,

FOUNDED ON TENNYSON'S POEM OF "ENOCH ARDEN."

BY

S. N. COOK,

AUTHOR OF "OUT IN THE STREETS," "BROKEN PROMISES," "UNCLE
JACK," ETC., ETC.

———————

CORRECTLY PRINTED FROM THE PROMPTER'S COPY, WITH THE CAST OF
CHARACTERS, COSTUMES, SCENE AND PROPERTY PLOTS, RELA-
TIVE POSITIONS OF THE DRAMATIS PERSONÆ, SIDES
OF ENTRANCE AND EXIT, DISPOSITIONS
OF CHARACTERS, ETC., ETC.

———————

NEW YORK
Copyright secured 1873, by
HAPPY HOURS COMPANY,
No. 5 BEEKMAN STREET.

THE WANDERER'S RETURN.

——: o :——

DRAMATIS PERSONÆ.

Enoch Arden...
Philip Ray..
Peter Lane..
Dr. Winthrop..
A Sailor..
Annie Arden...
Miriam Lane...
Nappy Ralston...
Boy, (in Second Act, four years old; in
    Fourth Act, fifteen years old)........ } Enoch's *Children* {
Girl, (in Second Act, five years old; in
    Fourth Act, sixteen years old).......

———

COSTUMES.—MODERN.

From the commencement of the Drama to the end, eighteen years are supposed to elapse—Costumes and make-ups to be arranged accordingly.

———

PROPERTIES.

ACT I.

Plain carpet down. Chintz curtains on each side of bay window, R.F. Fireplace set complete, with mantel, S.E.R. Round table, with cover, R.C. Four old-fashioned chairs. Work-box and needlework on table for Miriam.

ACT II.

Scene I.—Curtains to window, T.E.R. Fireplace set, with mantel, T.E.L. Rug and arm-chair before the fire. Sofa, R.C., at back of stage. Table, R., before the window. Work-basket, and work materials in it, on table for Annie. Toys for the two children to play with at back of stage. Pipe and tobacco for Enoch. Foot-stool.
Scene II.—Nil.
Scene III.—Plain garden seat, T.E.R. Table, L.C. Three garden chairs. Rustic garden arm-chair near table. Small profile full-rigged ship discovered at back of scene, U.E.R. Boat-truck and oars. Laurels, &c. Flowers in tubs round cottage.

Cradle up stage, L.C. Water pump fixed R.C., opposite second entrance. Large water-tub, painted green, on stand at back of cottage, L. Signal-gun, to fire from the profile ship. Lock of hair fixed up in a small piece of paper. A large brown paper bundle, corded, behind cottage, L.

ACT III.

SCENE I.—Two tables, R C. and L.C. Six chairs. Feather duster. An old and large umbrella for NAPPY RALSTON.
SCENE II.—Nil
SCENE III.—Curtains drawn apart to C. window. Round table, with cover on it, R.C. Lamp burning on table. Four chairs. Family Bible on table. Blue fire for two visions.   •

ACT IV.

SCENE I.—Broker pump fixed S.E.R. Shutters up to cottage window, L. Signboard hanging out, in bold letters, "FOR SALE." A short and old form, L.C. A broken stool, R.C. Broken paling, U.E R. A bundle of straw strewed over the stage in front of paling. Broken implements, &c., in various parts of stage, betokening wreck and ruin.
SCENE II.—Nil.
SCENE III.—Table and cover. Four chairs. Work-box and needle-work on table for MIRIAM.
SCENE IV.—Set quickly behind the gauze scene on its discovery. Large round table with cover on it. Lamp burning. Four chairs round table. Books for four in the circle to read. White curtains wide enough and long enough to open in centre, fixed behind window.
SCENE V.—Nil.
SCENE VI.—Cot with coverings, for ENOCH ARDEN to die upon, placed R.C. Table with cover, on the right of the cot. Large Bible upon it. Medicine bottles, basin and spoon, jug of water, glass, &c., on table. Chairs.

SCENERY.

ACT I.

SCENE.—

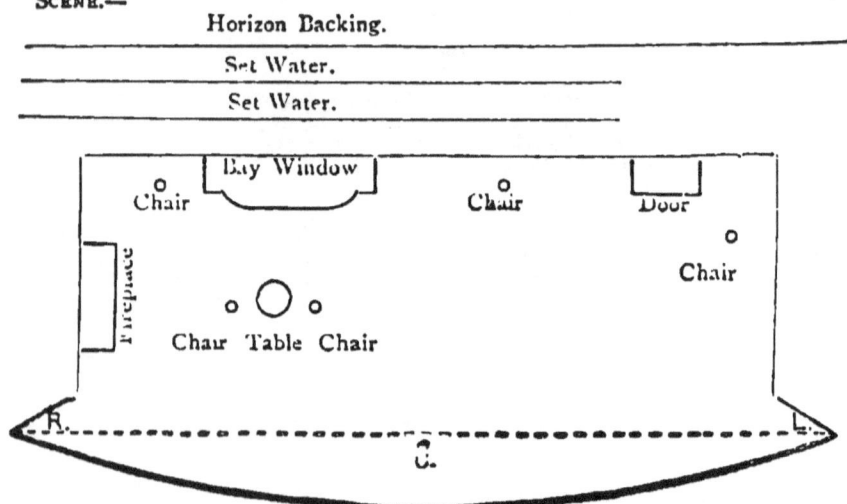

Interior of LANE'S Inn.   Large bay window, R F.   Door, L.F.   Fireplace set S.E.R. Table and two chairs, R.C., before window.   Three other chairs.   Set waters and horizon backing seen behind the window.

ACT II.

SCENE I.—

Interior Backing.

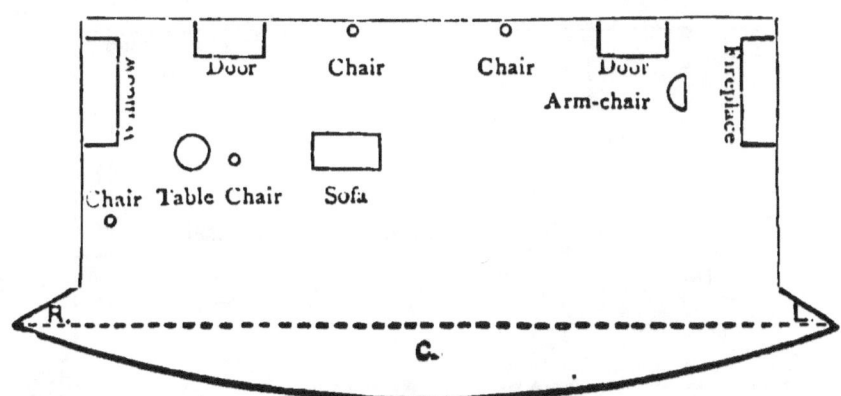

A Chamber at ENOCH ARDEN'S.   Doors R.F. and L.F.   Window U.E.R.   Fireplace set U.E.L.

SCENE II.—

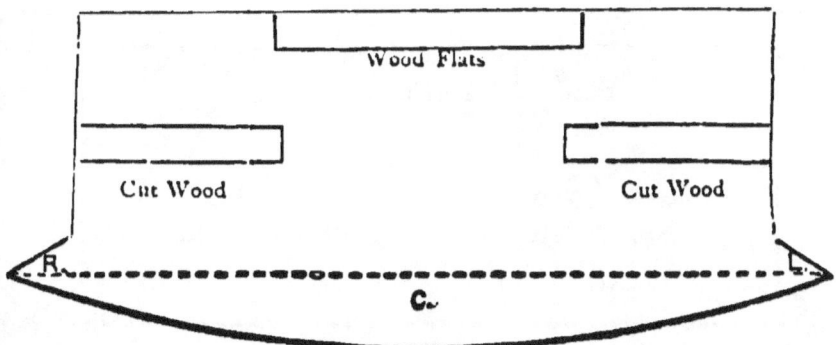

Wood and Cut Woods, in first and second grooves.

SCENE III.—

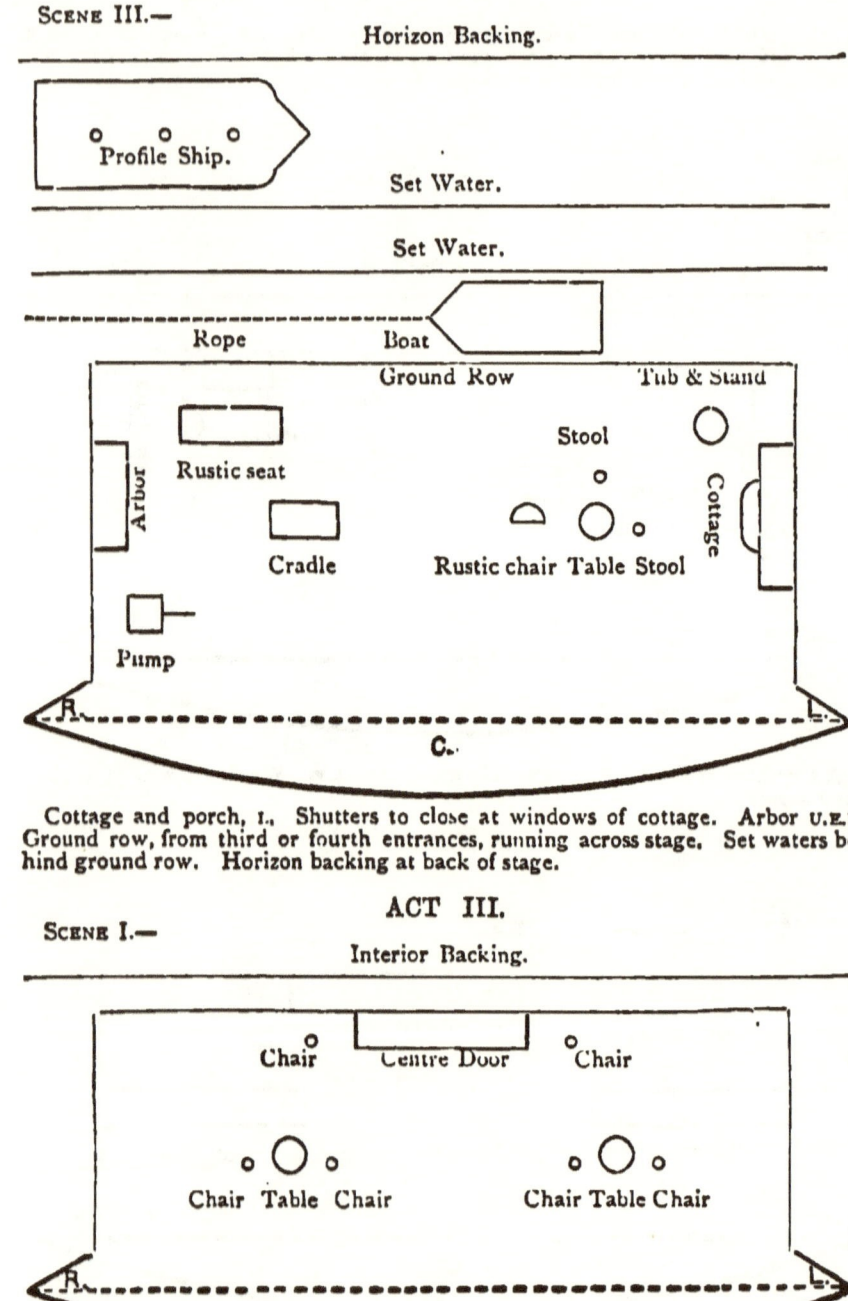

Cottage and porch, L. Shutters to close at windows of cottage. Arbor U.E.R. Ground row, from third or fourth entrances, running across stage. Set waters behind ground row. Horizon backing at back of stage.

ACT III.

SCENE I.—

Interior Backing.

A Centre Door Chamber at LANE's Inn—Second grooves   Tables and chairs, R.C. and L.C.

SCENE II.—

Interior Backing.

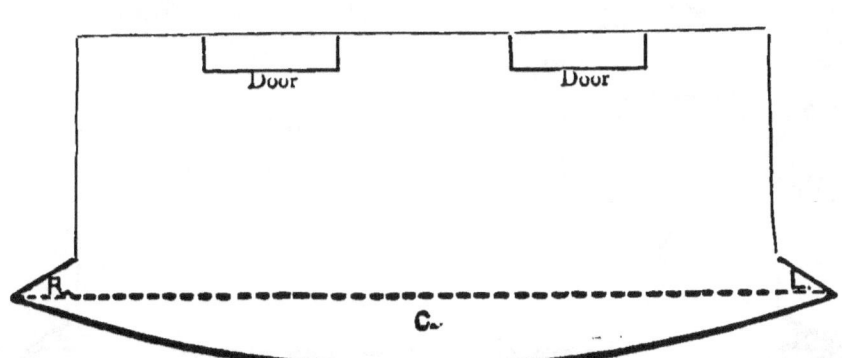

A Chamber at DR. WINTHROP's—First grooves. Doors in R. and L. flats.

SCENE III.—

Horizon Backing.

Set Water.

Set Water.

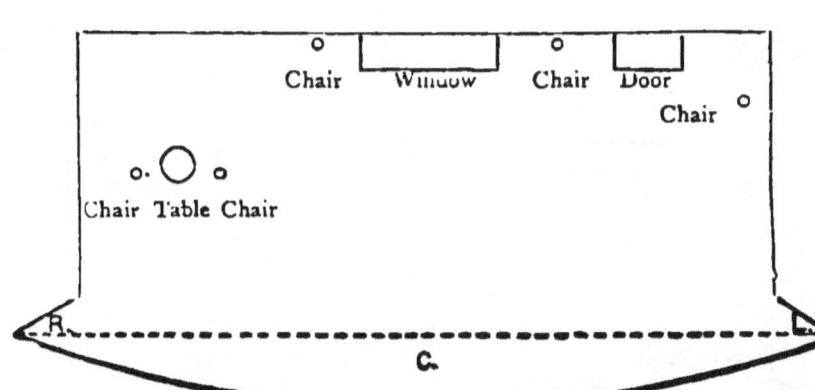

A Chamber at ENOCH ARDEN's. A wide latticed window, to open, in C. Door L.F. Set waters behind window. Horizon back of waters. Third grooves. Table and two chairs, R.C.

THE VISIONS IN SCENE III—

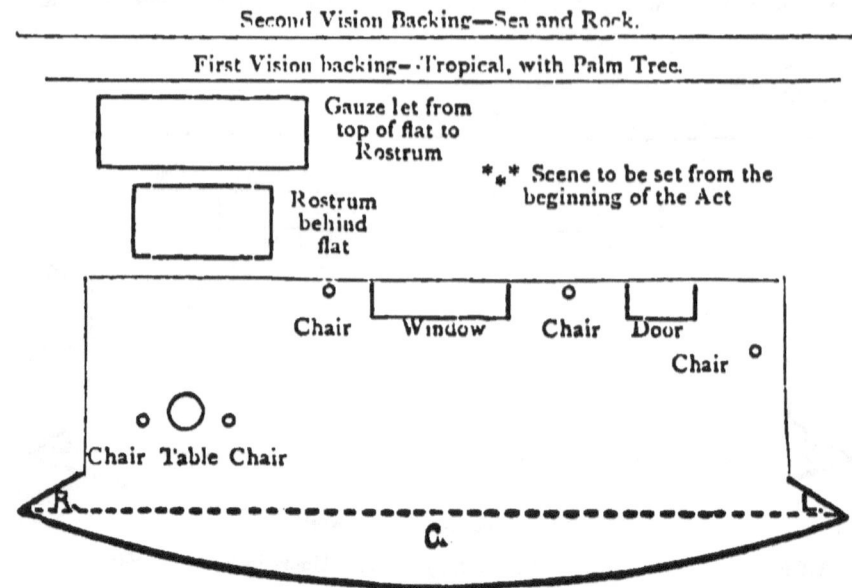

Second Vision Backing—Sea and Rock.

First Vision backing—Tropical, with Palm Tree.

Gauze let from top of flat to Rostrum

₊ Scene to be set from the beginning of the Act

Rostrum behind flat

Chair   Window   Chair   Door
                                   Chair

Chair Table Chair

R.   L.
                     C.

As seen through a gauze let in at the top of R. flat. Rostrum to reach the bottom of gauze. The first vision—at the beginning of Scene—tropical scenery to be used —a palm tree necessary. The second vision—at the end of act—marine and rocky scenery required.

ACT IV.

SCENE I.—

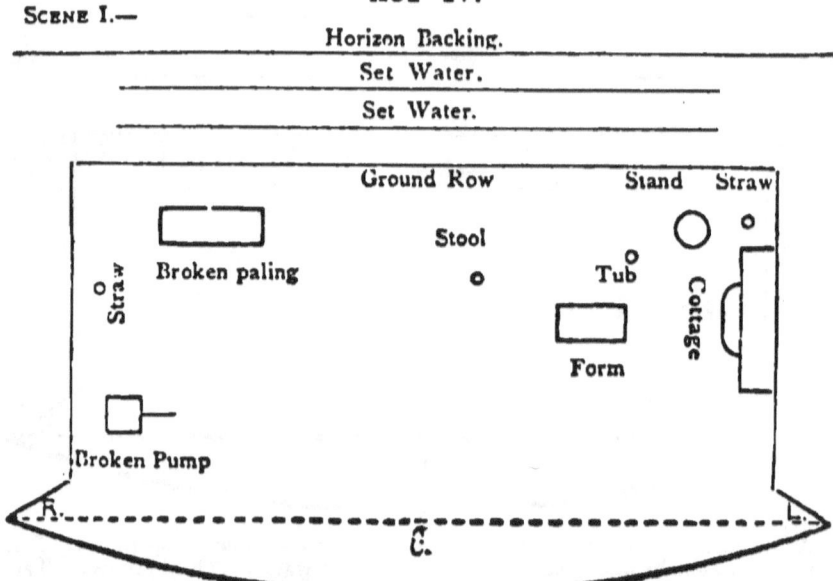

Horizon Backing.

Set Water.

Set Water.

Ground Row   Stand   Straw
Stool

Broken paling   Tub

Straw

Broken Pump

Form   Cottage

R.   L.
                     C.

Cottage and porch, L. Shutters to windows closed. Signboard hanging over door with the words "FOR SALE" Broken paling, U R.R. Ground rows from third or fourth entrances running across stage. Set waters behind ground row. Horizon backind at back of stage.

SCENE II.—A Front Wood—First grooves.

SCENE III.—

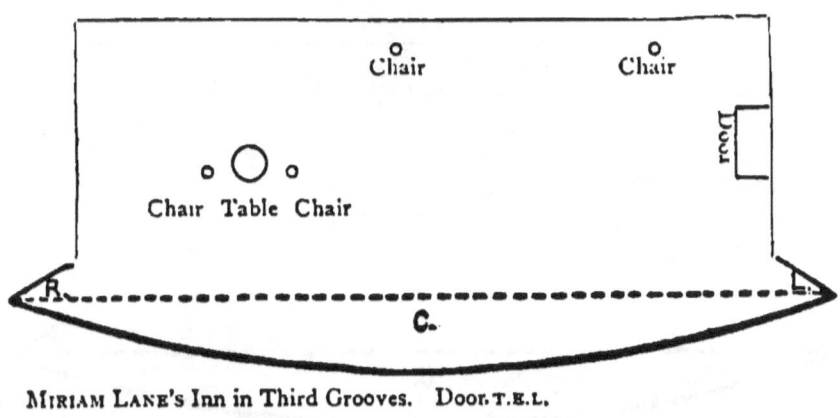

MIRIAM LANE's Inn in Third Grooves. Door. T.E.L.

SCENE IV.—

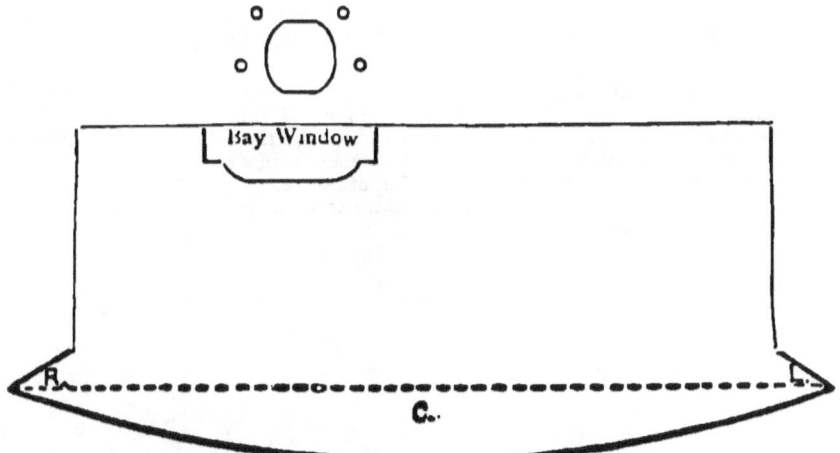

PHILIP RAY'S Cottage on the Outskirts (Garden Surroundings) in First Grooves. A large bay window with white curtains down. Behind the window a chamber backing.

SCENE V.—A Front Street—in First Grooves.

SCENE VI.—

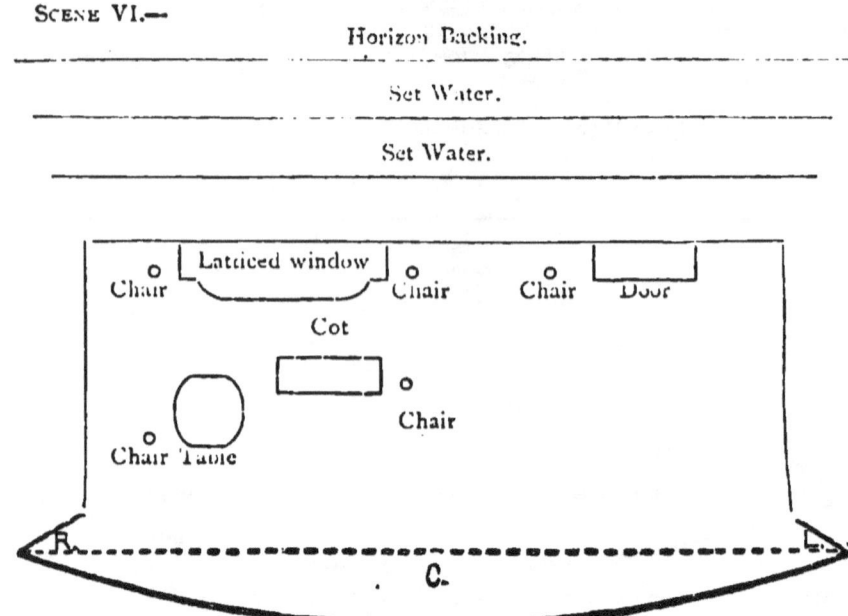

MIRIAM LANE'S Inn. Wide latticed window, R.F., through which is seen the sea and horizon beyond. Door in flat, L.

EXPLANATION OF THE STAGE DIRECTIONS.

R., means first entrance right, and right. L., first entrance left, and left. S.E.R., second entrance right. S.E.L., second entrance left. T.E.R., third entrance right. T.E.L., third entrance left. F.E.R., fourth entrance right. F.E.L., fourth entrance left. U.E.R., upper entrance right. U.E.L., upper entrance left. R.F., right flat, L.F., left flat. R.C., right of centre. L.C., left of centre. C., centre. C.D., centre doors. C.R., centre towards right. C.L., centre towards left. Observing you are supposed to face the audience.

THE WANDERER'S RETURN.

ACT I.

SCENE.—PETER LANE'S *Inn. An apartment with a large bay window,* C., *overlooking a rocky sea-coast, with horizon beyond.* Door *in* L. *flat. Fireplace,* T.E.H. *Old-fashioned plain tavern furniture. Music as curtain rises.*

MIRIAM LANE *discovered working at* R. *of* R.C. *table.* DR. WINTHROP *passes window from* R.

Enter DR. WINTHROP, *door* L.F., *and attracts* MIRIAM'S *attention by coughing—she, hitherto absorbed in thought, starts.*

Dr. W. (L.C.) Madam Lane, excuse me for troubling you; but can you tell me where I'll find your husband?

Miriam. (R.C.) Oh, Doctor dear, how you made me jump! I thought, perhaps, it might have been my husband (*Sighs.*) But no such good fortune. I think by this time you would have known that in some ale-house handy by you'd find old Peter Lane.

D. W. Ugh! The rogue! He well deserves the hangman's rope for treating such a wife as Miriam Lane is known to be, with such great disrespect.

Miriam. Oh, Dr. Winthrop, you know not what it is to possess a wife's anxieties, her cares. (*Sighs.*) You know not, indeed, what it is to be a wife! (*Places her work on table, and comes down* R.C.

Dr. W. That's very true! *(Aside.)* And at my time of life, I don't think it at all likely I shall ever become one.

Miriam. Always to be obliged to listen to the drivelling talk of one whose tongue is always too thick to wag with ease, caused from drinking too much village tap-room ale.

Dr. W. Ah, he's a sad old rogue *that man of yours:* I must believe all that the gossips of the port have said.

Miriam. And what, pray, have the gossips of the port now said of me or *him?*

Dr. W. Oh, not much, 'tis true ; only that the industrious Miriam Lane deserves a better man than the tippling Peter Lane, and which I also think is very true !

Miriam. *(Bristling up.)* And I would like to know what business have the gossips of this port to meddle with affairs of mine or of my husbands? And what right have they to wag their tongues about *this man of mine?* *(Goes to table and sits.*

Dr. W. *(Whistles—aside.)* A pretty mess I came near making here. I sympathize with her or tell her what the gossips say and she berates me sadly. Ah, they're all alike, these women folk, the whole world over, there's no difference in 'em. A man they've sworn to love they will abuse themselves most shamefully sometimes, but let another person say a just word against him, and then the war begins, and all the fat jumps out of the frying-pan and hops into the fire ! *(Places his forefinger on side of nose.)* I'm very glad I ain't a wife !

Miriam. *(Comes down* R.C., *from table.)* I'd have them know, Dr. Winthrop, that Peter Lane is my husband, and his drinking is my business—my business only—and his own, not theirs. They'd like to make disturbance with him, would they ; but they sha'n't. So if they want to make any disturbance with anyone, why let them come and make it with me !

Enter PETER LANE, *door* L.F.; *he is somewhat inebriated.*

Peter. (L.) Who's makin' a disturbance, wife?

Miriam. *(Rapidly crosses to him.)* You are Peter Lane. *(Arms a-kimbo, and shakes her head at him.)* You are always making a disturbance, for you are always drunk, you hog ! But little do you care for what the people say, or little do you care for the feelings of your poor wife, so that you can have your fill of grog, you—you, kilderkin. *(Cries.*

Peter. Why, wife, you wouldn't have me go back on the importance of any great event, would you? I'm sure I never drank except on great occasions.

Miriam. Oh, dear! You've had some great occasion, then, most every day in the year, and every year since we've been wed, and that's now nigh gone upon thirty! Why, you sulphurous "ne'er do well," you are so full of swill that if you only looked at a match you'd go off into a state of spontaneous combustion and set the house on fire, that you would. *(Shakes her head at him, with arms a-kimbo.*

Peter. *(Laughs uproariously.)* Well, that's a good joke, truly, wife. Upon my soul, I can't help laughing. *(To Dr. Winthrop.)* You see, friend Doctor, what a jolly wife I've got, and she makes poor me jolly too. Ho, ho, ho, ho! She's bound to have her joke if she dies for it, so that she can only play it upon me!

Miriam. *(Enraged.)* Joke! Joke, you brute? Yes, I *would* say joke if *I* were you! A pretty man you are for a brute. *(Scornfully.)* You—you hedgehog!

Peter. *(Holding his sides with suppressed laughter.)* Thank'ee, wife, I was allus counted han'som' when a boy.

(Grimaces in an inebriated manner.

Miriam. You'll be the death of me, I know you will.

(Cries and goes up c.

Dr. W. *(Comes down r.c.)* For shame upon you, Peter Lane, do you want to break your own wife's heart?

Peter. No, Doctor, that's too great an undertaking for a little fellow like me—I'm only dot and carry one. My wife is a b c, x y z, and all the etceteras.

Miriam. There, Doctor, only listen to him, just hear how he talks.

Peter. And how does he talk, my chickabiddy chuck? *(About to chuck her under the chin—She spurns him indignantly and bounces up the stage—Aside.)* My wife objects to being a chickabiddy. I'll call her an old hen the next time, see if that rooster'll please her better!

Miriam. 'Twould be all the same with him, Doctor, he wouldn't treat me any better if I were on my dying bed.

Peter. You'd have the last word then, old gal—hic—if you died for it—hic! But as I said just now I never drink except on great occasions, an'—an' important ewents; and I'd like to know if this isn't a gr-e-e-at occasion—hic—an'—an' an important e-went, when the bravest lad that rides the waves o' yonder bay takes for his wife the prettiest lass of all the port.

Dr. W. Well, said, Peter Lane; for once you've spoken words of truth and sense. Enoch Arden well deserves all honor we and every-one else can give him.

Miriam. That he does, for he is a good lad, a brave one and a true! And where is there a girl who deserves a better man than our Annie Lee?

Peter. No one! Not half a one! Not a soul among all the sane, unless 'tis our loving partner, Miriam Lane—hic!

Miriam. Will you hold your tongue, you fool?

Peter. Never mind her, Doctor, it's only a little way she has. It's not a way altogether in my way, but—hic—you know, I have to put up with it! And I say it now in awful earnest that she's a good woman—I may say a very good woman—Miriam is, especially when she's asleep; only at times she is awfully wide awake, and then she gets a little aggravated with her poor little husband, whose only fault on great occasions is that of getting too j–j–jolli-fi-carious and happy!

Dr. W. Take my advice, friend Peter, and drink no more!

Miriam. If he only would do that, Doctor, I'd never be such a scold.

Peter. Friend Peter hears—hic—friend Peter doth obey! Indeed you may take my word for it, drink—hic—is dead to me, and I never will, positively, never, never, never, *never!* Now listen, *(beckoning them to him)* while I take my pledge. *(Solemnly.)* I never will again, in all my born days, get jolly drunk—*(They congratulate and shake hands with him—He pompously folds his arms and walks aside,* L.)—except on great occasions and important—hic—e-wents!

Miriam. *(Hopelessly.)* Just as I expected!

Dr. W. Shame on you, sir, you'll break your poor wife's heart!

Peter. Now wait until I finish, will you? I said on great occasions and important e-wents; but there'll be no great occasions and important events come to this poor port, for Enoch Arden's married now, and times are growing duller day by day, for yonder town they are building only ten miles up the bay is taking all the trade from us, and we are dying slow but sure. There will be no more great occasions, no more important e-wents down here, consequently—hic—no more beer.

Dr. W. Then you will keep sober?

Peter. Just try me, Doctor, try me! Take me at my word—hic! This bitter pill *(tapping his breast)* to be chewed first and swallowed afterwards!

Dr. W. *(Laughing.)* I hope you will keep that pledge, friend Peter. But my errand here to-day is not to put a pledge on Peter Lane, although I hope it will be a good pledge sacredly kept. Enoch Arden and his lass—his loving wife—will soon be here. I have sent for them, and the surprise I have in store will make their young hearts beat and throb with youthful joy!

Miriam. Now, Doctor dear, do tell us what it is. I am not at all inquisitive, but I'd like to know!

Peter. Yes, dear Doctor, do tell us what it is. Look at us! We are not at all inquisitive, but we'd like to know!

Miriam. Don't keep us in suspense. Don't! *(Stamps her feet.*

Peter. Yes—no, I mean—don't keep us in suspense. Don't! *(Stamps his feet.*

Miriam. You always repeat after me every word I say.

Peter. That's because you allus say just the right words, my dear!

Miriam. Then hold your tongue, you old——

Peter. Darlin', my duck—that's the word you want to say, ain't it, my chick?

Miriam. *(Sneers.)* No it ain't, my goosey!

Dr. W. You want to hear what I've got to say, you queer people, and yet ye go to quarreling. Now hear me. You remember when the Earl of Brockland for a pleasure trip sailed down the bay, when a sudden squall upset his little boat, when he would have drowned had not Enoch Arden set full sail and ran his boat on some sunken rocks and saved him.

Miriam. Yes, I remember that.

Peter. Yes, I remember that, too! 'Twas a great occasion—an important ewent!

Dr. W. When you got drunk!

Peter. I should think I did, I never miss an ewent!

Dr. W. Now you all know that poor Enoch's boat was stove in by the sharp rocks she struck on, where Brockland's boat upset, and that it took the boy's past savings and future earnings to fix her right again.

Peter. I mind it well. I helped them fix her. Oh! and when we had finished her, with her new ribs—O-o-o! That was an ewent !

(Smacks his lips.

Miriam. Why, what could you do, pray?

Peter. What could I do? I did a good deal, and put away a good deal, I can tell you! You know he had to get a workman down from Lunnon, and that workman would have his pint of ale every hour. That fellow made an ewent for himself every sixty minutes!

Miriam. (*Sneers.*) And how did that cause you to help mend Enoch Arden's boat?

Peter. Why I carried the ale for the man, and held the jug which gave him stamina to prepare for the next coming ewent, didn't I?

Miriam. Peter Lane, you're an idiot!

Peter. Well, I know I'm next door to one.

(Moves a little away from her.

Dr. W. Don't interrupt me with such nonsense, sir. (*Resumes.*) We all thought the Earl of Brockland most niggardly for not offering to pay the lad for the breaking of his boat. The Earl merely thanked him, and rather gruffly too, and then went his way. (PHILIP RAY passes window from R.) Now here's a letter that I received from his lordship to-day.

Enter PHILIP RAY, *door* L.F.; *he crosses behind to* R. *corner.*

Dr. D. But here is Philip Ray! Come along, Philip, you're just in time, my boy. Come here, and listen while I read. (*Reads.*) "Dr. Winthrop—Dear sir, A young sailor named Enoch Arden saved my life last summer, and in doing so he not only risked his own life, but almost ruined his boat. I have had one built expressly for him, which in my name you will present to him, with my regards and best wishes for his future success and happiness in life. Yours, &c., Brockland." That boat (and she is a beauty, too) is riding now at anchor in the bay yonder. Enoch and his wife will soon be here, and this is the surprise I have in store for them.

Peter. (L.) And it's a glorious surprise. It's more—it's an event, and ought to be celebrated as one.

Miriam. (L.C.) Peter, hold your tongue!

Peter. I'm dumb *(claps his hand over his mouth)* as an oyster, and as close as one. *(Aside.)* Oh, I'd like to be an oyster! Them animals live on suction, and get fat upon it!

Dr. W. (R C.) Now, Philip, what do you think of this news?

Philip. (R.) That it is *good* news, but Enoch well deserves it, for he is brave, true, and honest. He may well feel proud of this new boat. I have seen her. and admire her—she's a beauty, and a prize worth the gaining. But it is only a painted boat after all. Not that nor all the boats or ships that ever sailed out o' yonder bay, or in or out of any port around the world can be worth one half as much to him as that other prize that Enoch's won—the heart, the love, the smiles of Annie Lee!

Peter. Oh, I've caught you, have I? You are there, are you? Yes, yes, you allus had a kind o' tenderness—a sort of 1 would if I could kind o' feeling towards that lass. Yum, yum!

Miriam. Peter, hold your tongue—you've said enough! Your judgment on such matters is none too good when sober.

Peter. I'm never too drunk to tell the truth, and with me you allus get it with the event.

Philip. You tell the truth, Peter, I'll not deny that. But you tell it in such plain, uncourteous words that it pains me. But I blush not to tell it. Annie Lee *was* all the world to me—aye, ever since she was a little lass and played at keeping house for us down by the bay. As children we have played together, as a child *I* loved *her!* But my love, my untold and secret love, has grown and ripened, strengthening with my years, my manhood. But I have uttered words here to you I never breathed to Annie Lee, for well have I known how hopeless was that one great wish of my desolate heart, ever since we all went nutting to the hazels in that Autumnal eventide, where she and Enoch sat there hand in hand together, so seemingly content in their little world, alone, beside each other, in the sunlight shadows of that lovely dell. Although since then there's been a lingering at my heart that naught can satisfy nor time appease, yet there is no malice lingering there—no, not even envy! Bless them both!

Dr. W. *(Shaking hands heartily with him.)* Spoken like a true man that you are, Philip. You may feel a little tender 'bout it now, yet there's many a happy day in store for Philip Ray.

(PHILIP *shakes his head.*)

Peter. Now, *I* wouldn't mind that kind of thing a bit, for she'll get old and cross some day, just like the rest o' plain married folk.

Miriam. Peter Lane, how dare you? Respect *me*, if you've lost all respect for yourself!

Peter. Oh, you're excepted, Miriam! *You*, my gem! Pooh! You're a jewel!

Dr. W. You two keep cool, can't you, and don't let your anger rise so suddenly. A few of such tempestuous outbursts 'twixt an old married couple like yourselves would be a bad example for a young and happy pair like Enoch and his wife.

Peter. That is the blessed truth you're telling again, Doctor! There's nothing like following a bad example—I mean a good one—and as I once heerd a fellow say, follow my precepts but not my bad example, I've thought of it ever since. *(Aside.)* And I am going to celebrate that ewent some day.

Dr. W. There, there! say no more about it, Peter. Your words are not likely to mend matters.

(ENOCH ARDEN *passes the window, from* R., *arm-in-arm with* ANNIE.

Dr. W. Besides, there's Enoch and his lass coming, Let us greet them cheerfully.

Peter. Aye, that we will; and you too, Philip! We're not the fox and the grapes, are we?

Miriam. Peter!

Peter. Oh, Lor'! *(Aside.)* That's a sour grape!

(PHILIP *appears annoyed, and turns aside,* R. *Music.*

Enter ENOCH *and* ANNIE ARDEN, *door* L.F.

Dr. W. Well, here you are, my children, obedient to my summons, Now that you are here, both of you, I scarce know how to begin, or what to say. 'Twas not to call a blessing down upon your heads that I brought you hither, for, you know, the dominie did that when ye were wed, and the good man's blessing will last you while you live!

Peter. And so it ought to, I should think, *all* your lives—and a day over—for he was long enough about it, wasn't he? So long, in fact, that I got nervous, and I began seriously to think I would have to celebrate the ewent. *(Yawns.*

Enoch. *(Laughs.)* With a drink, good Peter?

Peter. Well, I haven't got over it, yet.

Dr. W. Enoch, I have a letter here that is of interest to you, and I claim your kind attention, friends, while I read it. First, I'll ask you, Enoch, on your way hither did you see a new boat at anchor in the bay?

Enoch. That we did, and a new and handsome one she is! A beauty!

Dr. W. Attention, then! *(Reads the letter.*

Enoch. That new boat lying in the bay yonder for *me?*

Dr. W. Aye, for you, my man, and I've the honor, from His Right Honorable Lordship, the Earl of Brockland, to present it to you, Enoch Arden, as a slight recompense for your gallant endeavors in saving his lordship from the perils of the deep and a watery grave.

Annie. Oh, Enoch, ain't that grand? Can it be true? I almost fear the Doctor does but jest.

Peter. It's *jest* as true as gospel, every word.

Miriam. Peter!

Peter. *(Hand to mouth—Aside.)* Oyster!

Enoch. 'Tis a noble gift, and one I can well be proud of.

Dr. W. But you deserve it, my lad, for you justly earned it. What say you, my girl, do you share your husband's joy?

Annie. I do, indeed, Doctor! I am proud of the gift, but prouder of the owner who possesses it.   *(Embraces* ENOCH.

Peter. So am I! I'm proud of everything and everybody! I'm proud of myself!

Dr. W. *(Laughs.)* Your wife won't say as much for you, Peter.

Peter. Ah, well, as you're a spinster—no, I mean a bachelor; it's all the same—and hav'n't a wife, you can't appreciate the quiet blessings of a married home! *(To* MIRIAM.*)* Can he, my chick?

Miriam. Peter!

Peter. *(Same business.)* Oyster!

Enoch. I am anxious, friends, to see this boat of mine. A jolly sail we'll have in her down the bay, and you are all to go. And, Philip, you shall be the captain for the first cruise, and Peter Lane shall be the crew for the event.

Peter. *(Shakes his head,)* No, no, I fear it would not be safe, my lad.

Enoch. Why not, old friend?

Peter. The crew might all get drunk.   *(All laugh.*

Dr. W. Who'll christen her? The boat must have a name.

Peter. Let's call her "Peter Lane!" What do you say, wouldn't that be queer?

Miriam. Very! But she wasn't built to float in beer.

          (All laugh.

Peter. Was I built for that purpose, wife? That's a settler!

Miriam. You've drank enough beer and ale to float a whaler!

Dr. W. There you two go again. The boat must have a name. What shall it be?

Philip. The owner says I shall be the captain on this her first trip. Now, if I *am* to be the captain, I should like to christen her—then, when I take the helm, I shall guide o'er the mighty deep and land in safety the living cargo of the vessel, by whom I was called upon to name her!

Enoch. Annie here shall say who'll name the boat. Mayhap she's got a name to choose herself?

Annie. No, no, dear Enoch! Let Philip Ray name the boat!

Philip. That's soon done! *(Raises his hat.)* I'll call her "The Annie Lee!"

Omnes. (*Together.*) "The Annie Lee!"
 (PHILIP *becomes immediately dejected.* DOCTOR WINTHROP *noticing the movement, rouses him, forces him to take his hand, which he grasps, and points to Heaven, that* PHILIP *may gain inspiration and courage.* ENOCH *and* ANNIE ARDEN *embrace,* C.

Enoch. My young wife!
Peter. (*Embracing* MIRIAM *in imitation of* ENOCH.) My old woman! (MIRIAM *turns upon and beats him.* Tableau. *Music.*

ANNIE.   ENOCH.
DR. W.   C.
R.C.
PHILIP RAY.   MIRIAM.   PETER LANE.
R.   L.C.   L.

END OF ACT I.

Seven years are supposed to elapse between the First and Second Acts.

—◆◇◆—

ACT II.

SCENE I.—*A Room at* ENOCH ARDEN'S. *Doors* R.F. *and* L.F. *Window,* T.E.R. *Fireplace,* T.E.L.

ANNIE ARDEN *discovered working at table, before window,* T.E.R. ENOCH ARDEN *smoking—with both arms resting on his knees—close before the fire,* T.E.L. *The two children* (ENOCH'S) *playing with toys on floor at back of stage,* C. *Music.*

Annie. (*Dropping her work.*) It is of no use, I cannot work. My eyes grow dim with suppressed tears and my heart throbs and beats nigh to bursting! (*Looks round, and watches* ENOCH, L.) And there sits Enoch smoking and moping, and making himself wretched, with his knees almost upon the bars of the burning fire! There's something on his mind—I know there is—something, I fear, that he wants to tell me, but is afraid to do it. Why should he fear to meet me with unpleasant news, for am I not his wife, the mother of his children?

Enoch. (*Aside.*) Oh, how can I break it to her?

Annie. Yes, yes, he suffers! I know it—see it—yet his brave heart rebels at the mere thought of making me a sharer in his troubles! (*Rises.*) I will force him to lessen the weight from *his* mind by letting me bear the half of it *away* from him! (*Looks through the window.*) What is that I see? Enoch's vessel—"The Annie Lee" —(*hand upon heart*)—with strange colors flying—a strange crew on board! They weigh anchor—they set sail—"The Annie Lee" is leaving the bay. What can this mean? (*Goes suddenly over to* ENOCH, *and contemplates him—he sighs again.*) Enoch! (*She speaks to him again—but louder—laying her hand upon his shoulder.*) Enoch!

(*He starts—turns—recognizes her—takes her hand and kisses it.*

Enoch. Is that you, Annie dear?

Annie. Yes, Enoch, it is me. Are you unwell?

Enoch. Oh, yes, I am well—quite well!

Annie. Yes, yes, you may be in body. I hope, also, you are in mind, dear Enoch!

Enoch. (*Rising.*) Why, Annie, my darling, what ails you? What strange fancy has paled your cheek?

(*He leads her over to the* R.—*They sit*—ENOCH's *arm around her waist.*

Annie. Are my cheeks pale—so *very* pale—dear Enoch?

Enoch. And your eyes are red, and—an—merciful Heavens! they are filled with tears! What is it, Annie?

Annie. (*Placing her arms around his neck.*) For you, dear! I cannot see you suffer and not feel for you, not feel *with* you, for are we not man and wife—are we not one?

Enoch. (*Embracing and kissing her.*) Bless you, my pretty one —(*Sees the children silently playing up* C.)—and my poor little ones! (*Turns aside.*

Annie. (*Rises, and with vigor.*) Enoch, what is it? There is something on your mind? Tell me, your wife, I implore you—I insist!

(*Extends her arms and clasping her hands, as if entreating him.*

Enoch. Well, then, Annie, I—I—(*Turns aside*)—no, no, I cannot tell you, 'twould break your heart!

Annie. Then let it break! I have shared your joys, now let me wed your sorrows!

Enoch. (*Clasps her to his breast, and kisses her.*) Well, then, as you must know all sooner or later, perhaps the sooner the better! Know, then, that I have sold the boat!

Annie. (*Breaks from him.*) Sold the boat? That dear old boat you loved so well; which Philip Ray named after me! Sold "The Annie Lee!" Why, Enoch Arden, what strange fancy possessed you —what caused you to sell your boat?

Enoch. For the sake of you, Annie Arden, and these our little ones, I sold "The Annie Lee!" For well you know that since that fall I got that lamed me so, when I lay helpless for months on a sick bed, and you, my tender-hearted wife, so kindly nursed me, another came here with *his* boat, the trade became divided betwixt us, which at best was scant enough for one. But now——

Annie. But now what, Enoch? What is there for us now to do since you have sold the boat?

Enoch. I'll fix up your front room all tidy like with shelves and counters, I'll buy a good new stock of grocery goods, and Annie Lee that used to be shall keep the store for Annie Arden!

Annie. (*Dazed.*) "Annie Lee that used to be"—(*Looks him full in the face)*—"shall keep the store for Annie Arden!" But you, Enoch, what are *you* going to do? Not leave me?

Enoch. Oh, I'll do enough, believe me, to keep the kettle singing, and the pot a-boiling!

Annie. I know you will, dear Enoch, but why answer me so strangely? All day long I've felt so gloomy like, so sad and downcast, as though I were going to lose you, and for good. Now tell me truly, husband, you're not going away from me, from our children, are you? You're not going to far off London, there to be lost to us forever?

Enoch. No, not to London, Annie. (*Smiles.*) Why, what ails thee, girl?

Annie. You are keeping something from me, Enoch, and I must, I will know the truth. Now tell me all, I pray you! By the mem'ry of your past and present love! By the love you bear your children, and the mother of them, I implore, beseech you, tell me!

Enoch. (*Aside.*) I've not the nerve to tell her, 'twould break her heart.

Annie. (*Despairingly.*) Enoch, Enoch, what is it you are keeping from me?

Enoch. Well, Annie, lass, I'll tell thee all. I tried to break the news to you yesterday, after I had sold the boat, but, somehow I had not the courage. (*He speaks calmly, and in the same tone of voice to the end of speech.*) A ship, China bound, sails from this port in just six days. (*At this, ANNIE, who is standing in front of a chair, R.. places her two hands upon her forehead, stares vacantly, becomes dazed and motionless, until ENOCH has finished speaking.*) The ship did lack a boatswain, and I have hired, Annie. For the sake of you and these I'll go. I'll go on this one trip, and if successful, go one other one; when I can come home to you a rich man, Annie. Think of that! Then can we educate our children as they ought to be, and give them a better bringing up than your parents children or mine have ever been, dear Annie! (*ANNIE falls listlessly into R. chair.*) Annie, Annie, speak to me! Oh, the blow has kill-d her.

(*He is rushing over to her side, when PETER LANE speaks loudly without—ENOCH, at the sound of his voice, quickly walks over*

*to the fire and sits—The two children leave their playthings and
exeunt door* R.F.

Enter PETER LANE, *breathlessly, door* L.F.

Peter. (*Shaking* ENOCH.) Oh, here you are, and alive yet? Yes,
real flesh and blood, and no mistake! (*Hits* ENOCH *a blow on the
back, which makes him start.*) What do you mean by frightening us
all? Nappy Ralston has told me all about it. That you had gone
to China, and had been eaten up by the Carnibblers—no, I mean
that you were going to China, and were going to be eaten up by
the Carnibblers—it's the same thing—it's a mere question of time!
Oh, to think of going over to that Carnibbers, out-of-the-way country
to be poisoned by oloe berries and then buried in a tea-chest! Oh,
don't, don't go, Enoch! You'd make a nasty cup of strong Bohea!
But if you do go, (*clenching his fists*) I shall get so mad, that if you
are eaten up, and I get to hear of it, I shall send my old woman off
to bed first, and then out of sheer vexation, go off myself and celebrate the ewent! (ENOCH *laughs in spite of himself, and shakes hands
with* PETER.) Ah, that's right! Now you're coming to, and we may
be happy yet, as the song says.

Enoch. No, no, it's too late, friend Peter! I could not endure the
chance of facing poverty, so I've shipped on board the "Good Fortune," bound for China, and I've sold "The Annie Lee!"

Peter. What! Sold your wife? Why, you are worse than the
Carnibblers! No, I don't mean that. When I say sold your wife, I
mean she who was your wife before you married her! No, no! I've
got 'em all mixed up—green tea, and mixed, and Bohea, and Carnibblers, and Annie Lees and Ardens! There! It's a conundrum—I
give it up! (*Sees* ANNIE, R.) Ah, there she is! I'll talk to her!
(ENOCH *stops him.*) Oh, asleep is she? Poor thing! Where sleep
is bliss, 'tis folly to be otherwise! And *I* won't give her any of your
bad Bohea mixture to wake her!

Enoch. But if you talk so loud, Peter, you *will* wake her.

Peter. Oh, that's it, is it? Then I'll speak in a whisper. (*Whispers very low.*) If you promise not to go to China, I'll go and celebrate the ewent! (*Winks at* ENOCH.) What do you think of that?
There's torture for you? Well, do you promise?

Enoch. No! I must keep faith, having pledged my word.

Peter. That's nothing! I've often wanted to pledge my word to
my old woman, but she won't take it! She says I've pledged it so
often that it's completely worn out, and that if I want to sell it for
what it is worth, I must go to the junk market! But this won't do!
I can't stop talking to you all day—I'm going to stop you from going
to China!

Enoch. No, no!

Peter. Yes, yes! I'll go and tell the captain you've got the small-
pox. That'll frighten him! (*Going—is pulled back by* ENOCH.) I'll

tell him you've got varicose veins in your head—that you're troubled
with a swimming there—and that you can't go up aloft for fear of
tumbling down into the hold!

(Breaks away, and exit door L.F., *leaving coat-tail.* ENOCH
turns at door L.F., *and contemplates* ANNIE *for a moment—she
is weeping, with her head buried in her hands, resting on the
table—then crosses over to, and sits by her side—takes her
hand.*

Enoch. Annie, dear Annie, don't take on so. The darkest hour is
always the one before the dawn. Only a little patience, and the sun
will shine forth gloriously for all of us!

Annie. (Looking up.) Enoch, there is no sun here in my home
for me. You were my sun, my light, my life! And you want to
leave me alone in darkness, and our poor dear children!

(Weeps silently.

Enoch. (Distressed and rising.) Oh, Annie, child, you unman
—unnerve—me, and unfit me for the duties of the hour! All will
happen for the best! Why will you thwart my wishes, oppose my
views?

Annie. (Rises.) Never since the hour we were wed, Enoch, have
I ever opposed one act of yours; but now, for the first time, you'll
have to listen to your wife's thwartings, and bear with her if she op-
poses you, for never, never will you ever get consent of mine to leave
your home and children, and go on such a trip.

Enoch. Consider, my word, my pledge is given, and the captain,
knowing me, has paid me an advance, which will enable me to provide for you till my return, by fitting up your store.

Annie. You can give that money back.

Enoch. Not now, it is too late.

Annie. It is never too late to do good. Oh, Enoch, give that
money back.

Enoch. (Turns away.) I cannot, my word is pledged.

Annie. (Pulling him to her—face to face.) Perish your word!
Would you keep that, which in the keeping would cause your children and your wife to perish? What is your word given *now* to the
oath which you gave me at the altar? Which would you rather keep,
the oath given to your Maker, or your bare word given to the captain
of yonder ship? *(Points to window.)* Oh, untie the knot, Enoch,
undo that fatal word; think of your long absence, and remain with
us—your children, and your wife!

*(Clasps her arms around his neck, and lays her head upon his
breast.*

Enoch. I have thought of all that, Annie, often and often since I
first set my mind to improve our fortunes by the taking of this trip;
and, oh, how bitter is the pain that fills my heart when I think of
leaving you, my child, you, my loving wife.

Annie. (*Pleadingly—looking up into his face, with her hands clasped round his neck.*) Then don't go, Enoch!

Enoch. (*Unclasping her hands, and casting her from him.*) Don't tempt me, woman! (*She turns aside, silently weeping, burying her face in her hands—*ENOCH *relents, gently takes her hands, and draws her to his embrace.*) Forgive me, wife, for speaking thus to you ; but your pleading with me tempts me so to break my word. For well you know I would not leave you if it were not for our future good. Come, cheer up ; think not so much of all the lonesome days you'll have when I am gone, but rather think instead of all the brighter ones in store for you when I come back a richer man.

Annie. (*Prophetically.*) Enoch, you never will come back!

Enoch. (*Shuddering.*) Don't, don't, lass! (*Rallying.*) Why, Annie, girl, I'm afraid that grief has turned your brain. It's wrong to talk and go on so, for well you know that He who watcheth o'er us all, can keep me just as safe and sound on you great rolling sea, as in this little anchorage at home, with you as pilot.

Annie. But there's storm and shipwreck on the rolling deep, dear Enoch, which we never fear in this little anchorage at home.

(*Lays her head upon his bosom.*

Enoch. You're calmer now, dear wife! (*Looks into her face.*) And, ah, you smile! (*Kisses her forehead.*) God bless you and our little ones. (*Embrace.*) You spoke about the long years that I'll be gone ; your thoughts were gloomy then. Just months, dear wife. The lad and you will count those months at first, and think them long, and then you'll count the weeks, and soon the days ; and before you know it, the brave old ship "Good Fortune" will come sailing up the bay, and like enough I'll find our dear ones playing in the sands on the beach, just like you and I were wont to play when we were boy and girl together.

Annie. Ah, Enoch, well I know you are talking only now to cheer me, and well I know you think it for the good of us and ours, that you should go on this long, perilous trip, but every hour till that one fixed for sailing I shall pray unceasingly that some good fortune may yet betide us, and you still be spared to stay with us at this our little anchorage at home!

Enoch. Pray rather for a speedy trip across the seas, dear wife, and my safe return to thee and thine, at this our little anchorage at home.

(*Music—*"Home, Sweet Home"—*The children come running in from door* R F.—ENOCH *embraces* ANNIE—*She rests her head upon his breast—*ENOCH *looks upwards as if invoking a silent blessing upon his wife—The boy stands by his father's side, looking up into his face—The girl sits on a stool by her mother's feet, and sympathetically and silently weeps with her. Tableau. Closed in.*

SCENE II.—*Wood and Cut Woods in First and Second Grooves.
Music.*

Enter PHILIP RAY, L.

Philip. Another year has gone it's course, while still increasing prosperity has fallen to my lot. Some men are industrious and sober, work hard and with a will, yet fail in adding to their store of worldly wealth. Others, equally praiseworthy, yet without using superhuman efforts, and all they lay their hands on turns to grist. *(Smiles.)* I am one of the lucky latter ones—still, for all that, I am not happy! *(Sighs.)* Man requires some incentive to exertion—some one to work, to live for—to build a home for himself, with one of the other sex to smile upon him in that home, to help him onwards with her silent approbation, and cheer him by her actions to accomplish greater aims! And yet, I am alone! Oh, Annie Lee, An—but no, it is not right to think of her. She is another's, and that other is my friend! Poor Enoch! He struggles hard, works early and late, still, withal, remains unfortunate! The grinding wheel of fate favors some, disfavors others! He *shall* let me assist him. Three times hath he refused my proffered aid, but the next effort and I will force my good offices upon him,

Enter PETER LANE, R., *wiping his eyes.*

Philip. Why, how now, old friend, are your water works rolling? You are looking sad.   *(Laughs.*

Peter. Yes, and I don't belie my looks. I'm an undone Peter!

Philip. I never saw you look so bad before in all my life.

Peter. I never felt so bad before in all my life.

Philip. Been a drinking, Peter?

Peter. No, I ain't been a drinking, Peter! I'm a weepin', Peter, and I think I ought to baptize the event wi' beer.

Philip. What! has the patience of the good wife given out at last? Ho, ho, ho!

Peter. "The patience of the good wife—ho, ho, ho!" What do you mean?

Philip. Why, has she been flogging her Peter like a mother would whip her disobedient little boy?

Peter. Philip Ray, do I look like a *baby* as would stand the like o' that? Ugh!

Philip. Ho, ho, ho!

Peter. I see you are joking! But jokes are out of place at this sad time.   *(Sighs.*

Philip. "At this sad time?" Speak out, old man, tell me what you mean.

Peter. Why, he's goin' off, and she's grieving out her life a'most, an' says he'll never come back.

Philip. Who is going off, and who is grieving out her life?

Peter. Well, Philip Ray, ye'r dumber and blinder now than when you were a lad. To think you didn't know that your old playmate, Enoch Arden, has hired as a boatswain on the ship "Good Fortune," and she sails from out this port this very day.

Philip. (*Surprised.*) What! Enoch leaves to-day. Parts from his wife, home, children, and again to follow the treacherous life at sea? But whither is he bound?

Peter. Aye, that's the trouble, man. That's just what makes me weep. Enoch's wenturesome, and he's wenturing on his fate. He's goin' to China, among the pig-tails!

Philip. To China? Well that's not a dangerous place or trip.

Peter. It's not the place or trip that's going to kill him, man, but the pigtails when he gets there.

Philip. You are talking nonsense, Peter.

Peter. No, I'm not. They'll gobble him first, and bury him arter in a tea-chest.

Philip. Gobble and bury a man in a tea-chest? Ha, ha, ha! Now I'm sure you have been drinking!

Peter. There you go! I can't give information to anybody, but what they say I have been drinking. Nappy Ralston told my old woman—I mean my wife—that the pig-tails are all Carnibblers!

Philip. Carnibblers! What's a Carnibbler?

Peter. Why, a gobbler! The pigtails eat a poor devil in China just like we would swallow an oyster on the half shell. Sometimes they eat bits on 'em fried and stewed, but generally as a rule they smack their lips over 'em raw. Oh, I'd hate to die and then be eaten by a Carnibbler! Ugh!   (*Shudders.*

Philip. (*Laughs.*) Cannibals, you mean—man-eaters! Well, Peter, be sure of one thing, that if ever *you* should get so far from home, there'd be no fear of the savages in their right minds trying to feast on you.

Peter. No, I'd be a little tough, I know; but then I'd do, (*sighing and half crying*) and I'd go down easy with Worcestershire Sauce!

Philip. But if ever any Cannibals *did* eat *you,* Peter, they'd gorge over you in your raw state, depend upon it!

Peter. Would they? Why?

Philip. There's so much liquor in your body, that if they tried to cook you you'd flare up, burn to a cinder, and there'd be nothing left of you to eat!   (*Laughs.*

Peter. Oh, don't be personal. You wound my feelings!

Philip. But you are misinformed, friend Peter. There are no Cannibals in China.   (*Laughs.*

Peter. Ain't there? Nappy Ralston told me so. That's what made me feel so bad. Ugh! Fancy them nibbling away at Enoch's limbs! I wonder if they'd quarrel over his wish bone?

Philip. (*Angry.*) Old man, don't let me hear any more such silliness, it is wrong to talk so. You've been drinking again, for all you took the pledge.

Peter. Yes, I know I took the pledge, Philip, and it was a great occasion, I can tell you, and, you know, that event had to be celebrated. (*Goes up a little.*

Philip. So Enoch leaves to-day. A sudden notion this. Leave Annie and the babes? (*Pause.*) What will they do? I would not leave them. (*Half aside.*

Peter. (*Comes down.*) You wouldn't, hey? No, I don't suppose you would. Nor would Enoch Arden leave them if he had a mill a grinding like you—a mill a grinding that brought in brass enough to keep them all with plenty and at home! Enoch loves them all too well for that. How brave and cheerful like he bears it, tho' his heart's a achin' just like mine's a achin' now for him. But there's one thing sure—no odds how long his ship may go about a driftin' on the sea, them babes o' Annie Lee shall never want for bread, not while Philip Ray controls the mill, (*shakes hands with* PHILIP) or Peter Lane and his good wife can run the Inn,

Philip. No, that they shn'n't, good Peter. (*Returns his salute.*) But I must go and say good bye to him. (*Crosses to* R.

Peter. Here! I say—come back! (PHILIP *returns.*) Do you know you cheered me up amazin' like, for I was sure that Enoch was a goin' where they'd eat him? Oh, and if they had a eaten him, and he'd a never come back we wouldn't never a known how they'd finished him, would we? And it would allus been a worriment on my mind, not knowin' whether the pig-tails had taken him on the half-shell, or had him broiled.

Philip. (*Going* R.) Don't be a fool! You'd drive a person crazy with such nonsense. Let me hear no more of it. (*Exit* R.

Peter. (*Calls after him.*) Well, you go on and say good-bye to him, and I'll go and fetch Doctor Winthrop, and together we'll cheer the lad up a bit before he goes. (*Cross to* L.) Oh, them pig-tails, them pig-tails! O-h!

(*Holds his nose and exit,* L. *Music*—"Home, Sweet Home"— *before discovering*——

SCENE III.—*Cottage and porch, with ivy growing up and around same,* S. E. L. *Arbor and garden seat,* T. E. R. *Large water tub, painted green, on stand at back of cottage,* T. E. L. *Pump fixed* R. C., *opposite second entrance. Ground row from* T. E. R. *to* T. E. L. *Set waters beyond. Horizon at back of scene. Profile full-rigged ship at back of scene,* U. E. R. *Boat and truck ready behind ground row off at wing,* T. E. R. *Table and three garden chairs discovered* L. C. *Cradle up up stage,* R. C.

ANNIE *discovered weeping on* ENOCH'S *shoulder outside of porch,* L.—
The two children discovered rocking cradle at back of stage, R.C.
*Tableau. A signal gun is fired from the profile ship after the music
of* "Home, Sweet Home" *terminates. All the Characters move—*
ANNIE *shudders;* ENOCH *folds her closer to his breast, and looks
round to the ship; the children leave their rocking, rise, and look in
the direction of the ship—their backs to the audience. A* SAILOR *in a
boat rows on from* T.E.R.—*stops* C.

Enoch. The signal gun, Annie! In an hour we shall set sail!
Sailor. (*Having laid down his oar, stands up in boat.*) Did you
hear the gun, Mr. Arden? We are getting under weigh. The captain sent me to convey you on board. (ANNIE *clings closer to* ENOCH.
Enoch. All right, my man, in ten minutes. Go indoors and
draw yourself a mug of beer.
Sailor. Aye, aye, sir!
    (*Jumps from boat and exits into cottage,* L. *The children follow
    him off, staring with wonder.*
Annie. Oh, don't, don't leave me, husband, it will kill me!
Enoch. Come, Annie, wife, be cheerful, and go pack my little
bundle, which I must take with me, and, mind ye, in that bundle put
some little treasure owned by each of you, which I will keep ever on
my breast, locked there as a remembrance of my wife, my home, and
little ones. Not that I can ever forget thee, lass—no, no! Not one
hour of the time that I'll be gone—let it be months, or even years—
but what I'll think of you and home, or of some blessed memory of
our married life! But the little keepsake that ye are going to give
me, will bring ye nearer like to me when I am far away on the
bright blue sea!   (*Embrace.*

Enter the two Children, running, from cottage.

Boy. (R. *of* ENOCH.) Oh, papa, papa, that naughty big man with
the black whiskers, who came in the boat and is drinking ale like old
Peter Lane, says he's going to take you away ever so far, and that
you will live in that big ship yonder. You're not going to leave
mother and the baby, are you, papa?
Girl. (L. *of* ANNIE.) Don't let him, mamma, don't! Oh, I shall
cry so!
Annie. (L.C.) You hear them, husband? Even our children
plead to you for their mother.
Enoch. (*Looking up.*) What is to be, will be! (*Moved.*) Go,
go, rock the baby, children, an—and kiss it for your papa! (*Children go up and do so. Wipes away a tear.*) They make me lonesome like. (*Turns, sees* ANNIE *crying.*) Don't, don't cry, my darling, for that will make me truly wretched. (*Kisses her.*) Oh, once
on the deep, great sea, when for days and weeks, and months, perhaps, I shall be away, I shall miss my little darling's pretty little

prattle. And, little do they heed the thought now that when I'm gone the sweetest music of all the world will be the ringin' o' their voices in my ear, or the memories of the times when they put their little arms around my neck and kissed me, and told me o' their troubles or your joys! But let me not think of it. I am talkin' sorry like when I would fain be cheerful and be glad. This voyage, by the will of Heaven, will bring fair weather yet to all of us; so keep a clean hearth, dear wife, a clear fire, and I'll be back—to your surprise, dear girl—long before you know it.

Annie. Oh, Enoch, you are wise, and you are good; yet for all your wisdom—all you goodness—well I know it, that when you part from me, when you leave this beach for yonder ship, I shall look upon you for the last time on earth—you will see my face no more.

Enoch. (*Shivers.*) O-h! You chill me to the bone! Come, Annie, cheer up before I go, and don't take this little trip of mine so much to heart, (*She smiles sadly.*) That's right, smile as you did use to smile, nor ever again allow that lovely face of thine so much to resemble woe!

Annie. (*Points to rustic arm-chair, c.*) Sit there, Enoch, in that rustic chair—sit there once more—which you so nobly fill, and take our children upon your knee. (*Music—*ENOCH *sits—*ANNIE *goes up and brings the children down—*ENOCH *takes the boy upon his right knee —*ANNIE *places the girl upon his left—*ENOCH *dazed.*) I want to see you sit and hold the babes once more, to look into their innocent faces once again, to clasp their little hands, and feel the youthful throbbings and beatings of their little hearts. Pray, pray, my little ones. (*She joins the girl's hands—the boy, looking at his sister, clasps his.*) For, oh, the thought is killing me, of this solemn parting they will ever think of in after days.

Enoch. What mean you, wife?

Annie. 'Tis the last time, husband, that you will ever hold your kith and kin!

Enoch. Don't, wife, don't! You make my heart ache. Do not drive me mad!

(*He starts from his chair, putting the children aside, and beating his forehead.*

Annie. Enoch, I do not want to make your burthen heavier than it is, for 'tis hard enough at best—but truth is truth! If I could only drive such thoughts away, if I could only feel that you were coming back—though it were years from now—I would not grieve so, but I cannot, cannot (*breaking down*) feel that way. (*Crosses to cottage, L.—Turns to him at door.*) I'll go and get your little bundle now, though all the time I'll feel as if it were your shroud that you have bid me now get ready!

(*Music ends—*ANNIE *exits into cottage, L.—The Children have gone to the cradle.*

Enoch. The good wife has given me quite a turn. A clammy

death-like coldness is stamped in beads of sweat upon my brow.
(Shakes his hand from forehead.)   There! I'm better now! Ah!
here comes old Peter Lane—the kind old soul—and Doctor Winthrop,
too!   They've come to see me off and cheer me up a bit.   *(Music.*

Enter PETER LANE *and* DR. WINTHROP, S.E.R.

Enoch.   Aye, welcome, friends!   You've come to cheer my girl—I
thank you—*(Shakes hands with the* DOCTOR*)*—she's well nigh broken-
hearted and low-spirited.
Dr. W.   We've come to say God speed to you, good friend, and
speak a cheering word of comfort to your wife.

Enter ANNIE ARDEN, *with bundle, from cottage,* L.; *she places the bundle on table,* L.

Dr. W.   And here she is!   *(Crosses to* L.C.*)*   We've come to in-
voke Heaven's blessings on you and yours, to wish you well, and see
all faces blithe and gay on the departure of your husband from our
bay.   Come, come, my lass, don't look so cast down—think better of
this sacrifice your husband makes; 'tis to benefit you and yours!   It
will not be long 'ere he returns, and then the joy of seeing him come
home with the fortune he going to work for will well repay the pangs
of separation now.   *(Leads her up, they talk aside,* L.

The SAILOR *enters from cottage,* L., *takes the bundle from table and
enters boat.*

Peter.   (R.C.)   Enoch, let me take your hand, good lad, and say
God speed you among the rest, for there's none of all this world have
I to love but Miriam, and although she's hasty and angered like sometimes, she's true to the core for all that.   *(They shake hands heartily.)*
So, if the love of one frail old bark that's almost wrecked will be of
any value to you on your onward course, take it, lad, it's yours!   May
Heaven bless you, boy, and prosper you in all your ways.   I'm grow-
in' old and shaky, and my beacon lights are nigh played out, and
when I see your form a fadin' out o' sight down yonder bay, *(shakes
his head)* I'll never set my eyes on your manly face again.   So, you
will take my last advice, and blessing wi' it.   Be a good man all your
life—*(whispers)*—don't take to drinkin', Enoch, as is the way with
sailors, for it often makes a sea o' trouble twixt yourself and *(winks)*
your old 'ooman—that is, your wife.
Enoch.   (L.C.)   Thanks, old friend, I'll heed your words—and
what ye said about your love for me I'll carry with me to the grave,
for ye have a kindly heart, old man!   *(Shake hands again.)*   Now
he whom ye have treated worse than all the rest—ye know well whom
I mean—old Peter Lane himself, will soon lie down and rest for good.
And if of that good advice you gave to me you'd only take a part it
would be a drop of joy in a cup nigh filled with sorrow.

Peter. I'll heed your words, lad, 'deed I will, even on great occasions and *(winks)* celebrated ewents.

(Another gun is fired from profile ship.

Sailor. *(In boat,* c.) That's the second signal from the ship, Mr. Arden!

Enoch. One moment more for leave-taking, and I'll be ready.

Enter PHILIP RAY, *hurriedly,* s. E. R.

Philip. Enoch, I but lately heard of your intended journey. If not too late, and money can straighten you in your difficulties, bind you to your home, your children, and your wife, why, I've been thrifty, and I'm rich, command my purse, 'tis yours!

Annie. *(Comes down,* L.C.) Thanks, Philip, 'tis a noble act, and we are spared the pain of parting. You are indeed a friend in need.

Enoch. (c.) But it is too late, dear wife, my word is equal to my bond : I thank you, Philip, notwithstanding, and never shall I forget you for your proferred aid.

Sailor. *(In boat—Impatiently.)* Mr. Arden!

Enoch. This instant. The hour now has come and I must go. Good-bye to all.

(ENOCH *hurries to boat—*ANNIE *screams, comes* R.*—*ENOCH *turns —They meet again in* c. *of stage and embrace—*DOCTOR WINTHROP *brings down the children,* L.

Enoch. Annie, Annie, cheer up, be comforted! Look to the children, for I must go. My time's expired. Fear no more for me, or if ye do fear aught, cast all your cares and prayers on Him—He, who holds the anchor of the world! The sea is His—He made it, and can destroy—preserve, as well as make!

Annie. Take this, Enoch. *(Gives small packet.)* 'Tis a lock of our dear baby's hair!

Enoch. *(Takes and kisses it.)* I'll bring this back with me, my girl, when with riches I return to you and home.

(Music—"Home, Sweet Home" *played with muted instruments until the act drop is down, when it is played forte.*

Enoch. And now, my babe's, good-bye.

Children. Oh, papa, papa!

(DOCTOR WINTHROP *passes them to* ENOCH, *who quickly kisses them and again leaves them to the* DOCTOR'S *care.*

Enoch. Annie! *(She runs from* L., *embraces him,* c.) You'll know the time when I'll come back. Your heart will tell who it is, and you'll be waiting on the beach to greet me!

Sailor. Mr. Arden!

Enoch. God bless you, my darling, God bless you!

*(He rapidly kisses her two or three times, leaves her, and hurries up into boat—*ANNIE *stands bewildered and dazed, at last staggers and is about to fall, when* PHILIP RAY *rushes forward and catches her, as she faints, in his arms. Tableau.*

ENOCH *standing in boat, which*
is moving away, R.C.

ANNIE *in* PHILIP'S *arms.*
C.

CHILDREN
crying, L.C.

PETER LANE.
R.

DR. W.
L

END OF ACT II.

Ten years are supposed to elapse between the Second and Third Acts.

—◇—

ACT III.

SCENE I.—*An Apartment at* PETER LANE'S *Inn.   Centre doors, backed*
by Interior.

Enter MIRIAM LANE, C.; *she has a feather duster and commences dust-*
ing the furniture.   Music.

Miriam.   Now for a nice little tit-bit of gossip, for the A1, first-
class at Lloyds, chief of all the magpie gossips of this port, is coming
here to cuckoo all the news to me, and she sent me word of the important event, so as not to take a body altogether by surprise.
      (*She sits down* R. *of* R.C. *table, stretches and yawns,*

Enter PETER LANE, *cautiously, from* C. *door.*

Miriam.   (Aside.) Here she is! (*Aloud.*) Ah! I hear you,
Nappy. (*Arranges her dress with her back towards* PETER.) You
can't deceive me, my dearee, and what a long time since you have
been to see me, my lovee! Why, it's days and days since you've
crossed the threshold of Lane's Inn. (PETER LANE *closes* C. *door, and*
comes down on tiptoe, sits in chair L. *of* R.C. *table.*) And I've been
worked to death almost since that time, for that old man of mine
won't help me work a leetle bit, for I tell you, Nappy Ralston, one

had better have no man at all than have such an apology of a thing like—(*Discovers* PETER—*screams*)—Ugh! you brute!

Peter. (*Sneers.*) Miriam Lane, do I resemble Nappy Ralston?

Miriam. One way you do, and that's in coming here when you are not wanted!

Peter. Ha, ha, ha! How Nappy would enjoy that joke if she heard it. But as for poor me, the time you'll want me most will be when you're getting me measured for a coffin! O-h!
(*Twinge of the gout.*

Miriam. (*Rises, with arms a-kimbo.*) Now ain't you 'shamed of yourself to talk like that to your loving wife?

Peter. No, I am not! Look at me! I'm like a ship that has weathered many a storm, and made the owner's fortun'. You're my owner! But now that I'm getting old and there's no more work to be had out o' me, and the dry rot's set in, why, you lay me up in ordinary, and let me go to pieces!

Miriam. Dry rot indeed, and go to pieces! Bah! No wonder, for a man to drink as much as you have done.

Peter. Don't a man get dry 'fore he drinks, else why would he drink? And ain't I like a ship—for haven't I made your fortune—I'd like to know? (*Thumps the table.*) I say ain't I like a ship that's carried many a cargo?

Miriam. Yes, of rum! Ugh!

Peter. I say I am like a ship (*thumps table*) with a copper bottom!

Miriam. And I say you're like an old simpleton (*thumps table*) with an empty head!

Peter. Bah!
(*They nig-nag and quarrel, one each side of* R.C. *table.*

Miriam. Shut up!

Peter. Hold your tongue!

Miriam. I won't!

Peter. I'll make you!

Miriam. You're a monster!

Peter. You're a——

Miriam. What, what, what? (*Jumping up from table.*

Peter. An old mermaid!

(MIRIAM *screams, and makes for him across the table.* PETER *protects his head with his arms while she claws at him.*

Nappy Ralston. (*Speaking outside,* C.) Drat you, you young scalawag. If you laugh at me, I'll——

Enter NAPPY RALSTON, C. *door, followed by a boy, who laughs at her—she hits him over the head with her large umbrella and drives him off—closes door, and comes down to* R. *table.*

Nappy. Here I am, my dearee! Lor' bless yer, give us a kiss!
(*Kisses* MIRIAM—PETER *coughs and turns aside,* L.

Miriam. Peter! *(To* NAPPY.) Sit down, Nappy, my love, you are looking weary-like and care-worn.

Nappy. Marry come up, and so I am, which the only wonder is that I've been able to get here at all. Just to think of where I've been to-day. At the Ward's, and at the Ware's, and at the Tompkins', and at the Simpson's, and the Smithses; and ye know what frightful talkers they all are, my dearee; they are every one, and no mistake, which they are! And all had troubles of their own to tell, and troubles of their neighbors, and troubles of everybody else and where they couldn't find 'em, they made 'em up on their own account, which they did; and the Wards and the Wares won't speak, and the Smithses and the Joneses have had a fight, and Jones has blackened Smith's eyes, and Smith has battered Jones' nose. *(Laughs.)* And Smith's daughter was a-goin' to be married to Jones' son, which marriage is a broken off in consequence, which it is! And at each place I'd have to sit and listen to their stories of their fightin', and their fussin', and their funnin', and their a-flarin' up—which they allars are! Oh, it's shockin', which it is!

(Fans herself wildly with her handkerchief.

Peter. And you didn't get a chance to say a word? What a pity!
(Laughs aside.

Nappy. As a general thing, Mr. Peter Lane, I'm a woman as talks but little, which I does; *(to* MIRIAM) which you know, my dearee! Don't you, my love?

Miriam. Certainly, my dear!

Peter. *(To* NAPPY.) Oh, then this call o' your'n ain't "*a general thing*," as you call it? *(Sneers.*

Nappy. You know, Miriam, my pet, how tiresome it is, and how provoking, to listen to the talkin', and the fussin', and the funnin' of such a lot o' gossipin' chatterboxes, which they are. The Tompkins' and the Simpson's couldn't say a word but some kind of a sort o' slander about Philip Ray; and you know, Peter Lane, that he's as goodish a kind of a sort of man *(turns up her nose)* as is to be found in this 'ere wicked world of our'n, now-a-days, as far as one can find by looking hard for. Now don't ye?

Peter. *(Uneasy.)* Come, I say——

Nappy. *(Goes on.)* Although, perhaps, he is a-trifling with the heart of Annie Lee—but he don't know for sartin that she's a widow yet, which I don't think she are, which I don't!

Peter. *(Rising.)* Now, lookee here!

Nappy. Oh, yes, I know ther's many o' our neighbors censure our dear darling Annie. The Simpsons do, and the Joneses, and the Tompkins; they all think she's too soon forgot poor Enoch, and she knows not whether he is dead or not, an' she ought not to be a' looking at anybody else, much less a-thinkin' on 'em. It's shocking, which it is! Ah, poor man! It would be a bit o' fun if he would only a come back suddenly, an' could be a fly on the wall, an' look at all their little manœuvorings, and astonish 'em all! He'd better a stayed at home than ha' gone to sea, unless it's true what I have heard, that she berated the poor man until he couldn't stand it, because he wasn't rich and couldn't keep her comfortable.

Peter. (*Stopping her gabbling.*) Hold on, for heaven's sake.

Nappy. (*Apologetically.*) Oh, mind you, I don't say that it's true myself. In fact, I don't believe it, for you know I am one as never talks about my neighbors, for 'tis not the way to do, for one as is a christain, which it ain't. I'm only tellin' word for word what people say to me, the backbiters! (*Fans herself with handkerchief.*

Peter. Well, well, old lass, let up, can't ye? Jabber, jabber, jabber! Now ye've got to stop for breath. You're not the fust that's come here gossiping about your betters; but I've heard enough of it. There's some o' ye as talks o' Peter Lane in some such strain, and calls him "that old drunken scamp." (NAPPY *denies in dumb show.*) Oh, yes you do; I know it! And as for being a sot, I'm nothin' o' the sort. I never drink except on great occasions and to celebrate events, and that will never be again unless it is when Philip marries Annie. And if he never does marry her, why the business is their own — it's none o' mine or your'n, *Miss* Nappy Ralston!

Nappy. (*Jumping up and tucking umbrella under arm.*) Jus' so, *Mr.* Peter Lane. But I must go! I never like to stay, and feel that I'm pertrudin', an' if I do stay I shall mortify. (*Goes up* C.) I know I shall.

Miriam. (*Stops her.*) Don't take offence, Miss Nappy, and never mind what Peter says. It's the beer as talks, not Peter! He likes to hear the sound o' his own voice when he's that way, that's why he provokes folks as he does.

Peter. (*Laughs heartily.*) Lord help the man as tries to hold his own with you two blabs.

Miriam. There are lies a-flyin' round this place in plenty; lies hatched out by them as has nothing else to do but hatch 'em. And then they're peddled round by them as has nothin' else to do. but peddle 'em, drat 'em!

Nappy. (*Bristling up.*) Yer meaning me, I suppose! Do you, mum?

Miriam. I said there were people here as did the like o' that, but I didn't say *you.*

Peter. But that shoe fits like a glove for all that.

Nappy. I thought you couldn't blame the likes o' me!

Peter. (*Aside.*) No more nor a fish would swim.

Miriam. Why, the Ardens and the Rays are friends of ours; and didn't Annie mourn for Enoch in the past? And she mourns him now, poor girl; and he, good man, he must be dead, for had he been living, long, long ago you'd a seen him back, you would.

Nappy. Well, I'm the last person in the world to say one word of harm of any one, or breathe the nasty tittle-tattle that I hear; much less against a friend like Annie Arden. Why, we were little girls together! (*Crosses to* L.

Peter. (*Laughs boisterously.*) Ha, ha, ha! "Little gals together!" That's the strongest thing in jokes I've heerd for years. Why, Miss Nappy, you must have been born twice. Ho, ho, ho! (NAPPY *indignant.*) You and my old woman here (MIRIAM *looks indignant*) were little chicks as growed up side by side together, but that's many years ago, and Annie Lee was born the year when we were wed. Ho, ho, ho!

(*The two women walk up and down the stage,* R. *and* L., *furious* —PETER, C., *holding his sides.*

Peter. (*To* MIRIAM.) Walk, Miriam, walk!

(MIRIAM *stamps her foot, and goes up and down the stage at a more rapid gait.*

Peter. Nappy, walk! Walk, Nappy, walk!

(*Same business with* NAPPY—PETER *roars afresh,* C.

Nappy. (*Down* L., *turns* PETER *round to her.*) Brute!

Miriam. (*Same business on* R.) Monster!

Nappy. (*As before.*) You're a heathen!

Miriam. (*The same.*) A Hottentot!

(PETER *bursts into another fit of laughter, which starts them up and down stage again.*

Nappy. To dare to talk to me! A woman at my time of life!

(*Checks herself.*

Peter. Yes, I know your age, for I had a notion once of marryin' you myself.

Nappy. Oh, indeed! You're the only one of us two as hed the notion then.

Peter. Yes, but 'twas only a notion, for I kept it to myself!

Nappy. Oh, I understand that fling! But many a better man than Peter Lane have I refused.

(*Tosses her head.*

Peter. No! I didn't think you ever had the chance!

(*Laughs and crosses to* L.—NAPPY *cries in* C.

Miriam. (R.) Don,t mind this man of mine, Miss Nappy, for he's never content unless he's guzzlin' somewhere with men, or wrangling elsewhere with women!

Nappy. Oh, bless you, I don't mind him, Mrs. Lane. No, no, I —I r—a—ther like it! (*Bursts out crying.*) The neighbors all say he's getting childish like and is in his dotage.

Peter. Hear the clackin' o' her tongue, now! Clack, clack, clack, quack, quack, qua—qua—qua—qua—quack, quack, quack!

(NAPPY *makes a blow at him with her umbrella*—PETER *laughs, and gets away from her.*

Nappy. Never mind, it'll keep! Good-bye, dear Mrs. Lane, and when I come to see you another time, I hope you'll be alone. Away —from—your—*sweet* Peter! (PETER *laughs—she holds up umbrella.*) But I don't bear malice! You only come my way, Mr. Lane, and have a social cup of tea all alone with me, and I'll make it strong, and sweet, and hot. (*Aside.*) I'd like to scald him! (*Aloud.*) With plenty of cream—the cream of human kindness! Ugh! (*She grins*

—Peter *laughs*—Nappy *at* c. *door, turns.*) Oh, I'd scratch his eyes
out! (*Exits* c.
Miriam. Peter Lane, I'm ashamed of you! You ought to know
better than to talk in such a way to a woman—a poor lone woman!
Peter. What! (*Laughs.*) Call that wild cat of a thing a woman?
A creature that comes into your house with slanders on her tongue,
to injure the reputation of honest folk, and blast the happiness of
one's truest friends? You ought to talk with more sense, Miriam!
Miriam. Hold your tongue, Peter!
Peter. I shan't, madam! A woman is only deserving the name of
woman when she knows how to respect herself, and has feeling
enough in her heart to feel for the troubles and the woes of others!
All else is leather and prunella! (*A sudden thought.*) I'll go and
celebrate the event! (*Runs out* c. *door, hurriedly.*
Miriam. Come back, you wretch! I'll tear your wig off for you,
when I get near you! (*Follows out* c. *door. Closed in.*

SCENE II.—*A Room at* DR. WINTHROP'S. *Doors* R. *and* L. *in flats.*
First Grooves.

Enter DR. WINTHROP, *door* R.F.

Dr. W. Before I am an hour older I will have a talk with Annie
Arden. The little store is running down, and well I know she hath
no means of replenishing her stock. There is another little matter,
too! I know I have no business meddling with the love affairs of
anyone, but Philip Ray could end this life of struggle and distress,
yet fears to speak to her, as she mourns so bitterly for Enoch. Poor
Philip! He loves her as ardently now as when they were children,
playing on the waste together; but Annie loves the memory of the
husband dead these long, long years. But she ought to let that go:
her present duty is to the living, and I feel it a duty on my part both
to the living and the dead to try and set matters right.

Enter PETER LANE, *door* L.F.

Peter. (L.) Well, and you're the man to set matters right, Doctor.
And while ye'r in the business of a rigtin' up o' things, I want a lot
o' doctor's stuff to set me right.
Dr. W. (*Laughs.*) Some doctor's stuff to set you right, Peter?
Put out your tongue, man, and let me see the trouble that's on your
stomach.
Peter. I needn't show my tongue for this affliction. It's tongue
that caused it. I know ye for a learned man, Doctor, and if ye can
stop other people's tongues from cacklin' and a-gossipin' about their

betters, you would do a might of good and cure the feelin's that's a-troublin' o' me now.

Dr. W. Ah, man, I can do no good in such a case, It's only death can stop the clacking of the gossips.

Peter. But you're the doctor here, and look'ee what a chance you've got to stop this brood of cacklers! If I were the doctor in this town, see how I'd hurry death along for some on 'em.

Dr. W. You would not do that any more than I. You would not harm a worm, good Peter!

Peter. Wouldn't I? I'd crunch 'em under my big number ten. *(Stamps his foot.)* But these worms are feminines, and can cackle as well as crawl. The parson said the other day that every lie they tell is goin' to be set down agin 'em. Now to think o' all the lies they's tellin' round o' Annie Arden and her troubles. Oh!

(Strikes the top of his hat in.

Dr. W. Never mind them. There is not throughout all England one of England's daughters that hath been a better wife, or a truer to Enoch Arden, or his memory, than our dear Annie. Yes, Peter Lane, sometimes I feel a burning and an ugly feeling firing up this heart of mine when I hear some of the trash and gossip of the lazy ones, about that friend of ours who is sleeping neath the waters of some Southern sea, whose head is pillowed, perhaps, on a little mound of sand at the bottom of the mighty deep. The sand that's ever moving silently, but surely; that sand that's covered softly o'er his body like a funeral shroud. I feel it deeply.   *(Moved.*

Peter. Yes, and the little fishes all a-eatin' on him up! *I* feels it deeply.   *(Wipes his eyes.*

Dr. W. *(Crosses to L.)* I shall go talk to Annie now, and to these gossips I'll drop a hint or two that may blossom and bear fruit. Don't heed their tales, good Peter, nor listen to their talk, for there's a time for righting up the troubles of us all!   *(Exit L.*

Peter. It would take a long time to right up my troubles. If my old 'ooman would stop her clack, I could make a shorter cut. *(Uses handkerchief.)* But I think I'll go and celebrate the ewent.

(Follows out L.

SCENE III.—*A Room at* ARDEN'S. *A large open latticed window, in* C. *of flats, with curtains drawn apart, through which is seen the sea beyond. Gauze for vision to be seen behind, let in at the top of* R. *flat. Door in flat* L.

ANNIE ARDEN *discovered* L. *of window, looking through. The reflection of the moon is upon her figure. Music.*

Annie. Ten long years have passed away and still my Enoch comes not. Oh, my husband, father of my children, how have I mourned your loss. Yet will I not believe you dead, though all try to dissuade me still hope lives strong within me! The sea is calm and placid—almost as smooth as glass—and the moon shines brightly. Such a night as this it was on the eve when my husband left me! Ten long weary years and no ray of hope, no sign, no word of the living or the dead! How strange and weird and death-like seems this stillness all above and around the mighty deep! *(Opens the window and looks out.)* Not a murmur—and the air is hot and sultry. The faintest ripple of the waters alone can I hear as they break in little bubbles o'er the shingles on the beach. *(Closes the window and draws curtains.)* There! I'll look no more, but try to calm my wearied thoughts by reading, to while away my loneliness. *(Leaves the window and sits at table, R.; she turns up the lamp. Music played from the time of the window closing until the lamp is turned up.)* How wildly beats my heart, and a feeling doth come o'er me almost akin to terror, for I see the form of Enoch before my eyes continually. *(She opens the Bible.)* How earnestly have I prayed for a sign, that I might know if he be dead. I'll seek for one in this, the Holy Book, where all must go for help or consolation. *(Tableau. Music played through dialogue—muted instruments—until the vision is over. She places her finger on a verse in the Bible.)* "Under a palm tree!" What is there in that for me? Under a palm tree! *(Becomes dazed.)* Yes, I see Enoch—he waits for me under a palm tree. Under the palm tree that grows by the river of life! *(She leans her head upon the table, weeping. Lights arranged quickly before and behind the scene, when the vision is seen behind gauze over R.F., disclosing ENOCH under a palm tree, in the same dress as the one worn on the day of his departure. Tableau—Music ends.)* Oh, Enoch, Enoch! *(Starts up wildly, and looks round tremblingly at the place where she saw the vision—shrinks.)* Where am I? *(Feels the Bible, lamp, &c.)* Yes, in my own room. *(Runs quickly to window, draws curtains apart, looks out, and pulls them to again.)* There is nothing there, and yet I saw him plainly, as on the day of his departure! *(Comes back to N.C. table—seems bewildered.)* When will this mystery end? *(Giving way to her feelings.)* Oh, Enoch, Enoch, come back again to me, and end this agonizing misery!

(Falls in chair, and buries her face in her hands—weeping at table.

Enter PHILIP RAY, *door* L.F.

Philip. (At doorway.) There she is, poor girl, ever fretting and sighing, wearing her young life away! *(Closes door and comes down.)* Annie, I—*(Going to her, stops)*—but no, she is nervous, and I might frighten her. *(Advances quietly and calls her.)* Annie, Annie Arden!

Annie. (Looking up wildly.) Who's there? *(Sees* PHILIP—*places her hands in his.)* Oh, it's you, is it, Philip?

Philip.   Still weeping, Annie?   *(Shakes his head.*

Annie.   I've been looking for a sign, to know if he be among the living or the dead!

Philip.   *(Aside.)*   Will she never give up looking for the one that's dead?   *(Aloud.)*   Annie, the ship in which your husband sailed was lost.

Annie.   Yes, the ship was lost, but the crew?   Are they all gone? I have my doubts.

Philip.   He whom ye loved so fondly and so truly, Annie, is now——

Annie.   *(Stops him quickly.)*   Don't, don't say that word, friend Philip!   I've been searching for a sign in this the Holy Book, to know if he be dead.   My finger rested upon these words, "Under a palm tree!"

Philip.   Ah!   Then you think that he is——

Annie.   With the blest!   *(Looks reverently above.*

Philip.   Annie, can I speak?

Annie.   Speak?   *(Looks at him.)*   Speak, friend Philip.

Philip.   Annie, there's a subject shackled upon my mind, and it has been imprisoned there so long, that, though I know not how or whence it first became enslaved, I feel that it must be set free at last. It is against all chance, beyond all hope, that he who left you ten long years ago should still be among the living.   You say yourself that you believe he is with the blest above.

Annie.   *(Hopefully.)*   And yet he may be among the living, Philip!

Philip.   It cannot be, Annie!   Oh, if you but knew how I do grieve to see you poor and wanting help, and I cannot help you as I could wish to do—unless—they say that women are so quick—perhaps you guess what I would have you learn—I wish you for my wife then, Annie, and fain would prove a father to your children.   I do think they love me as a father, and I am sure that after all these sad, uncertain years we might be still as happy as any of His creatures.   I have loved you long, and silently, and ardently, dear Annie.   Then, think upon it, for I am well to do, no kin, no care, no burthen. Then let me bestow my care upon you and yours.   Be a husband unto you, a father unto your children!   We have known each other all our lives, dear Annie, and I have loved you longer than you can well remember.

Annie.   You have been as Heaven's good angel in our house, and He will bless you for it.   But you are worthier of some one happier than myself!

Philip.   No, Annie, no!   Place yourself under my charge and guidance, let me soothe your sorrows—I will convert them into joys. You are the friend of my childhood, the love of my riper years, and are the only one I want.   You chose the best among us years ago, dear Annie, but he is gone.

Annie. Can one love twice in one life, Philip? Can you be ever loved as Enoch was?

Philip. I will be content to be loved a little after Enoch.

Annie. Dear Philip, wait a little. For should Enoch ever come——

Philip. Enoch will never come!

Annie. *(Giving way to despair.)* No, no, he cannot come, he has been too many years away! But, Philip, wait another year. One year is not so long to wait. Surely I shall be wiser in a year. Oh, Philip, wait a little, for my sake! Do!

Philip. I am used to waiting, Annie, for I have waited all my life for thee, and surely I well may wait a little longer now.

(He turns to go—she calls him—he stops.

Annie. *(Reaches her hands toward him.)* Philip, you have my promise—in a year *(he takes her hand and kisses it)* I will be thine!

Philip. Oh, Annie, Annie, mine at last. *(She weeps, and sinks in chair at table—Aside.)* She is mine, yet why does she weep? Aye, 'tis for the one that's gone. Her heart is buried with him—with the dead—in the deep bosom of the wide ocean. I do her wrong to wring from her a promise, and will retract. *(At doorway L.F.; calls back to her.)* Annie, Annie, *(she looks up and turns to him)* when I spoke to you of love—of marriage—it was in your hour of weakness. I was wrong. *(Going out at doorway.)* I am always bound to you, but you are free! *(Exits door L.F.*

Annie. No, I am now bound to you, Philip, *(rises)* at home, wide, far, or near. I'll be thy wife in another year!

(Music—"Home, Sweet Home"—muted. She falls kneeling at the chair, and praying. Lights arranged for second vision. ENOCH appears behind the gauze in the dress he will wear during the next act, surrounded by wild and rocky sea-coast scenery. Tableau. Act drop slow.

END OF ACT III.

One year is supposed to elapse between the Third and Fourth Acts.

ACT IV.

SCENE I.—*The Exterior of* ENOCH ARDEN'S *Cottage*, L.—*dilapidated. Shutters up to windows. Sign board hanging over door, with the words, "*FOR SALE.*" Horizon backing. Set waters and ground row. The water-tub*, L., *off its stand. Pump, broken,* S.E.R. *Broken paling,* U.E.R. *Lights half down. Music—"*Home, Sweet Home*" —played before the curtain rises and continued till——*

ENOCH ARDEN *enters* U.E.R.; *he is careworn, in tattered garments, and his hair and beard are grey; he sits on the old form.*

Enoch. (*Smiles sadly.*) Anchored at last—securely moored in the safe harborage of home! (*Looks round at back.*) Yes, home—that home which I left for parts unknown. (*Goes up* C.) Here floated the ship's boat which took me from the shore, and there, (*points to the horizon, on the* R.) that floating coffin, the ship "Good Fortune." (*Laughs.*) What a name! "Good Fortune!" I, who was once spry, strong, and lion-hearted, am now (*looks at himself*) but a mere wreck, bent and broken. (*He has come down stage, and is about to sit on the broken stool, which gives way; he moves away and sits on form; sighs.*) How strange I feel to-day! My hands are cold, (*rubs them*) my eyesight dim, and I—(*Stares vacantly*)—I can hardly see! (*Looks round to* R.) And the once bright colors that made our happy home look cheerful, they, too, seem dimmed with years, and (*looks again at his garments and sighs*) misty like its owner. (*Rises firmly and with outstretched arms, looks up.*) But I am home once more, home to Annie Arden and the dear children! (*Rubs and clasps his hands gleefully.*) Oh, won't my lass be glad to see me! (*Relapses.*) I hope she has not given me up for dead, for that would be more awful than all my sufferings! (*Smiles faintly.*) She'll not not know me though at first, I look so old, so broken down and grey-like. Oh, but I'll grow young again when I see my wife! That is, if *she* and the dear children are yet alive. (*Childishly.*) I'll go round now to the back the house, enter her small store, and sit there like a stranger waiting to be served, enjoy the joke, and at the last only, when I have teased them well, will I tell them who I am.
(*Pleased and chuckles to himself; he gradually moves down* C., *with his back to* ANNIE.

Enter ANNIE ARDEN (*Daughter*), *running and laughing, from* R.

Annie. (R.C.) He tried to catch me, and I ran away. Oh, what fun! (*Looks* R.) Here he comes!

(Turns to go L., *and meets* ENOCH *face to face—she appears frightened, trembles at his appearance, and remains rooted to the spot.* ENOCH *stares in a dazed and vacant manner, keeping his eyes fixed upon her features, as if endeavoring to bring them back to his recollection, when he places his fingers on his forehead and draws them away. Music—"Home, Sweet Home,"—muted instruments. They move round the stage— each one's eyes fixed upon the others—*ANNIE *first to* L., *when her face is full to the audience, then* ENOCH, *with his back to them—goes* L.C.—ANNIE, R.C.

Enoch. (*Sighs,* L.C.) She walks like Annie used to walk, and looks like Annie. (*Shakes his head.*) But no, no, no, she is too young! (*Sighs.*) Oh, my heart!

(He moves away, keeping his eyes fixed on ANNIE *until off* L., *when music ends.*

Annie. What a strange old man! He did so frighten me at first; but I don't there is any harm in him. Perhaps he was hungry. Poor fellow!

Enter PHILIP RAY, *from* R.

Annie. Ah, here you are, papa, and you've caught me, haven't you? That is, I mean, I've caught you! (*Laughing.*) And do you know I'm going to scold you? (*She takes his hand.*) And don't you think you deserve it?

Philip. (*Laughing.*) What for, my darling? What has papa Philip done?

Annie. (*Serious.*) Why, everything! Haven't you kept us waiting, and don't you think by that you've done enough? Isn't that sufficient to make mother oh, ever so mad?

(Smiles and shakes his hands heartily.

Philip. And is mother just as mad as you are, my dear?

Annie. Ah, now you are poking fun at me again. Well, never mind, if mother scolds, but I don't she will! (*Quickly.*) But if she does, I'll take your part. There?

Philip, You are an angel, Annie!

Annie. Oh, no, I'm not, papa, or I wouldn't have frightened a poor old sailor who was here just now.

Philip. A poor old sailor! Here?

Annie. Yes, papa. I was scared at first, but I don't think there was anything to fear from him. He might have been a shipwrecked sailor, for he looked woe-begone enough and ragged enough for one. I never saw a shipwrecked sailor; but then I've read about them, you know.

Philip. (*Aside.*) A sailor—an old sailor—shipwrecked?

Annie. What are you saying to yourself, papa Philip?

Philip. Nothing, my dear. I was only thinking. (*Muses.*

Annie. Thinking that that poor shipwrecked sailor was hungry, perhaps. *(Places her arms round* PHILIP's *neck.)* If he called upon us, and he was hungry, we'd give him food and shelter, wouldn't we, papa?

Philip. Yes, yes, my dear!

Annie. *(Looking after* ENOCH, L.) Poor old man! I do so feel for him. I hope he isn't hungry. *(To* PHILIP.) Oh, I wouldn't like you to go away hungry from our house, papa, if you were poor!

Philip. Come, come, my Annie, we must not keep your mother waiting. Let us go!

Annie. Yes, papa! *(Sighs.)* Let us go home!

(Music—"Home, Sweet Home"—*muted instruments.* ANNIE *looks back after* ENOCH, L., *her eyes almost filling with tears.* PHILIP *leads her off,* R., *she fixing her eyes in* ENOCH's *direction.*

SCENE II.—*A Front Wood.* "Home, Sweet Home" *continued from the previous scene until——*

ENOCH ARDEN *enters from* R.

Enoch. Wrecked in sight of port! Pilot house and pilot both are gone, and the danger signal flying at the fore—"For Sale." *(Mind wanders.)* Home! A-h! *(Sighs.)* Children and wife, like sire, wandered, perhaps, only to founder! Perhaps they are dead—dead —dead! *(Weeps.)* And *I* am here! Dead to kindred, dead to all the world! What is there for me to live for? Of all my friends— alike, if kith or kin—of those that stood upon the beach to see me leave, not one to give me welcome back again, or greet me to their shore, as I once so fondly dreamed they would in days gone by. All turned from, and all shunned, me, same as they would slink away from one whom they had long mourned as dead! That young girl, too! So like unto my Annie! *(Shakes his head.)* And yet, so tall, so grand! But, then, I've been away for years—wrecked and lost for years—and I've grown grey since I've been away; and yet, to have grown out of remembrance of one's own child! It's time that I were dead! Children, wife, babe, all gone! May the husband's turn soon come! House and store, too, dark, still, and empty! Ruin within, ruin without, and ruin at the heart! For in the dim, uncertain light, I read the sign outside what once was home, "For Sale!" *(Looks round.)* Where now can I go for shelter? What can I do, or where look, and to whom, for hope? I'll go to Peter Lane! *(Going.)* See there—if he be living—whether he also will shun and flee from me as dead? *(Exit* L.

SCENE III.—MIRIAM LANE'S *Inn.   Door* T.E.L.

MIRIAM LANE *(attired in mourning) discovered seated at table* R.C., *working.*

Miriam.   Dearee me, how lonely all doth seem to be, surely, now that my poor Peter is no more.   Ah!   He often said I'd be the death of him with my tongue ; but, Lor' bless me, 'twas the nasty liquor he put down over *his* tongue that quieted him at last !   One can't celebrate so many ewents, as he used to call 'em, wi'out paying summat for the celebrations !   Poor Peter !   He's in his lone grave, and I'm left all alone to battle with the world as a lone widder !

Enter DR. WINTHROP, *door* T.E.L.

Dr. W.   (L.)   Well, Widow Lane, you are all alone, I see !
Miriam.   (R.C.)   Yes, Doctor, all alone !   Only my needlework to keep me company.   (*Sighs.*
Dr. W.   (*Sighs.*)   It's catching !   (*Sits* R.C.)   I have been to see the ailing sick, and humored all their whims ; and now I have a little time to chat with you, fair widow, for well I know that you are lonesome now that he is gone.
Miriam.   Lonesome ?   That I am !   There are not many stopping at Lane's Inn these days, and oh, the time it really seems to move so slow and dreary-like.   Why, the longest days of all my life have been the ones that have passed since Peter Lane was laid away to rest.
                                                            (*Puts down her work.*
Dr. W.   I doubt it not !   Your old man—I mean poor Peter—had his failings, as we all know, but then he was a jolly soul and carried round with him, where e'er he went, as kind a heart as one could find throughout all England.   (*Moves nearer to her.*)   But what's the use of mourning or of fretting 'bout him now, dear widow ?   Grieving never brought a soul back into the world, and the pleasures of life (*sighs*) are for the living, not the dead.
                                                            (*He twiddles his thumbs.*
Miriam.   I'm not a grievin' or a frettin' over him, Doctor.   I was only talkin' of my lonely lot in life !
                                 (*She looks at him, sighs, and then twiddles her thumbs.*
Dr. W.   (*Looks round approvingly, and gets nearer to her.*)   You keep a nice public house here, Widow.   What an obnoxious term that is of widow ?   It seems like a counterfeit, and ought to be changed for good !   (*Sighs and gets closer to her—she sighs.*)   There ought to be a man in charge of this same house, dear widow !
                                                            (*Twiddles his thumbs.*
Miriam.   I know that, dear Doctor.
                                 (*Looks up at him, and twiddles—they both sigh together.*

Miriam. O-h, Doctor!

Dr. W. You are still young.

Miriam. O-h!

Dr. W. Good looking!

Miriam. O-h!

Dr. W. Buxum!

Miriam. O-h!

Dr. W. Ripe!

Miriam. O-h, Doctor!

Doctor. You want plucking, widow!   (*Sighs.*

Miriam. Doctor, you make me blush!

Dr. W. Blushing and ripe, red and rosy, charming widow. Then why don't you marry again?   (*Puts his arm round her waist.*

Miriam. (*Her face close to his.*) But who will I marry, Doctor?
                                                      (*Sighs.*

Dr. W. Hey? Why, marry the first good man that asks you.

Miriam. I've made up my mind to that, but it has done no good so far. They're backward in coming forward, Doctor.

Dr. W. Well, then, charming and adorable widow, I've been thinking that——

Enter ENOCH ARDEN, *door* T.E.L.

Dr. W. Bother! Here's a customer!   (*Rises.*

Miriam. Don't be in a hurry, Doctor, he may not mean to stay. (*Aside.*) When he was coming to the point, too! How provoking!
                                     (DR. WINTHROP *goes up stage*

Enoch. Can I find lodging here for the night, good madam?

Miriam. You can. No traveller ever asks for shelter or for food at Lane's Inn, but what he gets it, that is, if he in looks be decent-like at all. Are you a traveller and a stranger in this port?

Enoch. (c.) A traveller? Yes! But I am no stranger. I've been in this port before.

Miriam. (R.C.) A traveller by land or sea?

Enoch. I've just come off the sea. (*Aside.*) Miriam Lane and Doctor Winthrop—I know them well, but they know me not. (*Sighs.*) Am I then so changed?   (*Crosses to* L.

Dr. W. (*Listening at back,* L.C.) That voice! I think I've heard it somewhere before.

Miriam. Aye, like enough. He says he has been here to the port before,

Dr. W. It seems more like the voice of one I knew in days gone by, but who or where I cannot tell. I'll come again, good Mistress Lane.

Miriam. I'll look for ye. (*Exit* DR. WINTHROP, T.E.L.—*To* ENOCH.) You've been a sailor in your day, you say? That must have been many years ago, good friend, for now, I judge, your day is past, you look so old and feeble! Sit down and rest, old man!

Enoch. (*Aside.*) Old man, indeed! (*Aloud.*) I've been a sailor in my day, good madam, though, as you say, I'm broken down and feeble now. (*Sits L.C., and sighs heavily.*

Miriam. (*Aside.*) Poor man! He suffers much! (*Aloud.*) What a hard and toilsome life that of a sailor is, and full of danger, too. Is it not so?

Enoch. It is, indeed! A life on the ocean wave, a death under the silent deep!

Miriam. How many poor sailors go to sea that never come back again, Heaven only knows.

Enoch. Did any from this little port ever go away to sea, and never return, good lady?

Miriam. Yes, indeed, more's the pity, old man!

Enoch. Lately, may I ask?

Miriam. The last was about eleven or twelve years ago. No letter, no tidings! Ah, well, he must be dead!

Enoch. And his name? It was——

Miriam. Enoch Arden! (ENOCH *sighs.*) He was a fine stalwart young fellow, strong and hearty. You've been strong and hearty once, old man, and must know how proud it must make a body feel. (ENOCH *sighs.*) Well, poor Enoch was a friend of ours, and of my dead and gone husband, Peter Lane.

Enoch. Peter Lane—dead?

Miriam. Yes, it was a sad event.

Enoch. And an—Enoch Arden too?

Miriam. Both dead. Ah! He was a good husband, a loving father, an industrious lad, and the pride of our little port. Well, things went wrong with him, somehow, so Enoch—who used to have a boat here on the bay—hired as a boatswain on the ship "Good Fortune," bound for China. But the ship foundered, or was burnt, or something dreadful happened, as none of 'em ever come back to tell the tale. Before he left he sold his boat to provide a home and livelihood while he was gone for his wife and child!

Enoch. Ah! (*Excited.*) He had a wife, then?

Miriam. (*Surprised.*) Why, yes, poor man. Sailors *have* wives sometimes, don't they?

Enoch. Why, yes, yes! But is she well-to-do—is she alive?

Miriam. Alas! Poor Annie! (ENOCH *much moved—aside—at the mention of his wife's name. Slight pause.*) She seemed to prosper well at first, but grew low-spirited as month after month went by and no word came from Enoch. Then the youngest child——

Enoch. Yes, yes, the child!

Miriam. A baby!

Enoch. Yes, the little baby!

Miriam. In its cradle!

Enoch. (*Aside.*) God bless it!

Miriam. Well, it always was a weakly one; and it grew weaker and weaker like day after day, and at last the poor thing died.

Enoch. (*Screams aloud.*) Oh!

Miriam. What is the matter, my good man?

Enoch. A sudden pain here at the heart! (*Sighs.*) You know I
—I am so old and feeble!

Miriam. Ah! we none of us get younger, do we? Well, poor
Annie—that was his wife—how I pitied her, her heart was almost
broke, and her only cry was Enoch, Enoch—ever the name of her
dear husband. Oh, how she yearned for him the day the baby lay a
corpse. Old friend, you never saw a creature born of earth so beau-
tiful—like a little angel carved from marble—as it lay in its little cot,
so white, so cold, so sweet. And Annie sat there tearless with her
heart a-breakin', and a-thinkin' of her baby dead, and of her husband
dead and gone, and both in heaven! Why, you are crying, old man!
Don't cry!

Enoch. I cannot help it! I've been a husband and a father,
(*cries*) and know full well what it is to be away in distant climes
and lose a cherished little one at home!

Miriam. Don't weep, good man! That dead baby's living soul is
resting there above! Don't grieve, old man! I told Annie not to
grieve when her dear baby died, that it was wrong to fly in the face
of Heaven, and that Enoch and his dead baby were there together!

(ENOCH *unable longer to restrain his feelings, weeps aloud, and
takes* MIRIAM *by both hands.*

Enoch. Excuse these tears; but that poor dead baby!

Miriam. Why, you feel it as much as Annie did! Ah, I see *you*
have been a husband and a father! The best men seem to suffer
most!

Enoch. If that be so, judging by my present sufferings, then I
must be good indeed! (*Smiles bitterly.*

Miriam. Well, Annie waited and she watched, and no tidings
ever came. Year by year she fretted, and she pined, and wasted, and
grew thinner day by day. At last she too was convinced of Enoch's
death, and, in answer to the prayer of all of us, to rescue her from
poverty, and to save her life——

Enoch. Yes, yes, her life, yes——

Miriam. She married Philip Ray!

Enoch. (*Starts up.*) What, married? She married to another
while her first husband—— (*Laughs wildly.*

Miriam. (*Frightened.*) What is the matter, my poor man?

Enoch. (*Recollecting.*) Oh, nothing, nothing! (*With his hand
to his heart.*) Merely a touch of my old complaint. You know, I
told you I am so old and feeble!

Miriam. Ah, keep calm! Excitement is bad in extreme old age!
Well, Annie, dear girl, is happy in her husband's love, and with
Enoch's children living with them she is proud as well as happy!
(ENOCH *groans aside.*) Enoch—poor man—I've often thought about
him—but, then, I doubt not he was cast away and lost!

Enoch· *(Dazed, crosses wanderingly to* R.) Cast away and lost!
(Aside—solemnly.) Yes, yes, never to be found!

Miriam. (L.) He hath a tender heart, poor man! I can see the
tears now standings in his eyes, as though he knew and loved all
those that I have told him of. *(ENOCH sinks into a chair* R., *buries his
face in his hands, and silently weeps at table.)* I'll go and build a fire
in his room, for I noticed that he shivered so at times as though he
had a chill. *(Exit* MIRIAM, T.E.L.

Enoch. *(Rises.)* None of the old folks now know me. It is
well for me, and they never shall, for their own peace sakes! *(Cross
to* C.) I have not long to live—no—I feel that now—then why break
in upon her peace, only to mar it? She is alive, and happy! So
Miriam said, Poor baby tho' is dead! I soon shall start upon the
same long journey after her—the self-same road to follow with one
so blest. I've stranded upon this shore for death, but when I land
again there'll be a little one a-standin' on the sands across the river
waiting for me, and with her *(looks up)* 'twill be for life! But I
must once more see the dear ones that are left—my Annie—*(Checks
himself)*—no, no, not mine, not mine—but the boy and girl belong to
me. I must gaze on them before my mission ends, then for the veil
to all!

(Exit T.E.L. *Music—"*Home, Sweet Home*"—played till* ENOCH
is on his knees in the next scene.

SCENE IV.—*Enterior Flats of* PHILIP RAY's *Cottage—A front scene. A
large bay window in* R. *flat, with white curtains down—to open in the
centre at the proper time. Door of cottage in* L. *flat. The interior of
cottage to be backed by a chamber. Lime light on behind flats. Lights
down in front of stage from the opening of scene. See to the quick
setting of the stage behind flats, ready for the discovery, which is near
the commencement of the scene.*

ENOCH ARDEN *enters,* L., *he crosses over to* R., *gazes at the lighted window, turns away, looks again, then falls upon his knees in front of it,
and prays. Music—"*Home, Sweet Home*" ends here.*

Enoch. My jewels there, locked up; and I—the owner of them—
do not possess the key! It is hard to bear! *(Looks at window.)*
Open then, the precious casket, and let me look upon my dear ones,
ere I am shrouded in the grave! *(Clasps his hands.)* Thou that
didst uphold me as the last and only man upon that lonely isle, uphold me, Father, in my loneliness a little longer. Aid and give me
strength to withhold from her all knowledge of my presence here!

Help me not to break in upon her peace or cause my children sorrow! (*He buries his face in his hands before the window, and weeps. Music. The curtains are drawn gently up and aside from the centre, discovering* ANNIE ARDEN, PHILIP RAY, *and the two grown-up children seated at a table reading. Looks up.*) They are there, my blessed ones! She, my wife, and he—oh, let me not think of it, the thought is maddening! (*Rises, and runs to window. The curtain descends, closing the group from his view. He turns away in despair.*) What, must I not look upon or speak to them, my own? (*Music ends.*) There, there is no father's kiss for me! My girl so like her mother— my son, too, and not for me! Oh, Annie, Annie! Never will you know the truth, for never will I break your heart, as mine is broken!
(*He becomes unconscious, and sinks upon the ground.*

Enter DR. WINTHROP, *door* L.F.

Dr. W. (L.C.) I have passed a jolly evening with my friend Philip—and who has a better right to partake of his hospitable cheer than I? For have I not caused their happiness? Well, I just made her marry him, though neither of them have the least idea that I separately urged them on. (*Sees* ENOCH *on ground,* R.C.) What's this? Tut, tut, tut! Too bad, too bad! An old sailor—and drunk! Ah, those fellows when they get ashore never know when they've had enough! (*Shakes* ENOCH.) See here, old hulk, it's bad enough for one that's young to drink too much, but when an old fellow, with one foot in the grave, like you, gets drunk——
Enoch. No, no, not drunk! Unless my cup of sorrow is running o'er, then only am I drunk! A word!
Dr. W. You set a bad example for one so aged. I cannot encourage you. (*Exit* L.
Enoch. (*Starts up.*) Drunk! Ha, ha, ha! Is misery then so akin to drunkenness that there are but few judges left to detect the difference? (*Laughs wildly.*) It is time that I were gone! (*Calls.*) Here, Dr. Winthrop, I know you! You shall know me! Let me lay bare my heart, give vent to my woes, end all, and start on my pilgrimage to come! (*Exit, after* DR. WINTHROP, L. *Closed in.*

SCENE V.—*A Front Street.*

Enter DR. WINTHROP, *hurriedly, from* L.

Dr. W. (*Looks back.*) There's a mystery about that man! He was not drunk! Why, then, was he prowling around near Philip's door? Ah, he's following me! (*Going* R.

Enter ENOCH ARDEN, *suddenly,* L.

Enoch. Stay! *(Goes to him.)* Are *you* mad?
Dr. W. Mad? No! *(Aside.)* What ails the man?
Enoch. Then am I drunk? Answer me! *(Stamps his foot.*
Dr. W. No, no, no!
Enoch. I am! Drunk with misery and woe! DR. WINTHROP
going R.) Stay, I tell you! "Old hulk!" *(Laughs.)* I have a
word to say—a favor to ask from *you!* You'll be going back to that
house, *(points off* L.) where all seemed happiness within—where you
beheld misery—myself—huddled up in rags, without?
Dr. W. I shall be returning there!
Enoch. *(Commandingly.)* Say nothing, then, to them of the man
you saw crouching before their window panes. The blazing fire
within looked cheerful to this one homeless man without. The scene
recalled the times of other days, much happier then than now, and
with the feebleness of *(laughs satirically)* "my old age" I sank upon
the wet and muddy earth to rest! Say nothing to them of the event.
Do you hear me? Promise me!
Dr. W. I do promise, and will keep my word!
Enoch. Then farewell! *(Going* L. DR. WINTHROP *follows.)*
Don't follow me! You'll know me before I die! *(Exit* L.
Dr. W. And now the mystery's all the greater. But I'm promise
bound and must not say a word to Philip or his wife! But I will
follow him, discover who and what he is, and where he goes to.
(Exit, after ENOCH, L. *Music—*"Home, Sweet Home"*—played
until the discovery of——*

SCENE VI.—MIRIAM LANE'S *Inn. Wide latticed windows,* R.F., *through
which is seen the sea and horizon beyond. Door in* L. *flat.*

ENOCH ARDEN *discovered lying on a cot,* R.C. MIRIAM LANE *seated at
a table,* R.

Enoch. *(Writhing with pain on couch.)* Water, water! Oh, for
a drop of water to quench the thirst of a poor shipwrecked mariner!
(Falls back.
Miriam. *(Rises and helps him.)* Here, poor man! *(He drinks.*
Enoch. Thanks, thanks! (MIRIAM *places the glass on table.)* It
is almost over and I shall bear the secret to my grave! Oh!
(Groans.
Miriam. If it is a secret you have upon your soul and you feel that
you are going, leave it behind you, and spare pain to others. *(Tenderly.)* Dost hear, old man?

Enoch. I am not an old man! Is't because my hair, my beard is grey, my eye caverned, and my cheek blanched, you think that I am old? 'Tis with terror, pain, suffering! *(Hand upon his heart.)* Aged at the heart with sorrow, but young, though broken in my years of hope! Oh, Annie, Annie Arden! *(Suffers.*

Miriam. *(Starts.)* What—*who?* What know you of Annie Arden? Speak, I pray you!

Enoch. *(Laughs wildly.)* My secret's here, *(hand to heart)* and I shall bear it with me to my grave!

Miriam. Spare others, if *you* suffer. Be just!

Enoch. I *am* sparing *others,* that is why I keep my secret to my-self! Oh, if they but knew, their joy would vanish for all time! I shall not last long, and then it will be safe, safe, safe! *(Wanders.*

Miriam. No, no! Patience, and we shall bring you round. Ten-der nursing and careful watching, and you will be right again. *(Draws near to him.)* What of this secret and of Annie Arden?

Enoch. *(Vacantly and wildly.)* Swear upon this book, then, and I will tell you, but you must not divulge it till I am gone!

Miriam. *(With hand on book.)* I promise! There, 'tis sworn, and you need not fear for Miriam Lane.

Enoch. Enoch Arden—you knew him?

Miriam. Knew Enoch Arden? Why, yes, I told you of him—the sailor that was lost—held his head high and cared for no man in this port.

Enoch. That was the man! But now his head is low and body bent, and no man cares for him. I am that Enoch Arden!
(Exhausted.

Miriam. *(Shakes her head dubiously.)* You—Arden? Nay, nay, he was a foot higher than you are, my poor man he was young! You do but rave!

Miriam. I tell you, woman, that I am *he!* *(Very pathetically.)* God has bowed me down and bent my spirit to what you see me! Grief and solitude have broken body as well as mind, but I am that same Enoch Arden who married Annie Lee. *(Points to heaven.)* She whose name hath twice been changed by man, and both alive! *I* married the woman who, while I live to tell it, married Philip Ray!
(Pause.

Miriam. *(Slowly.)* And—you—are—Enoch Arden? *(He faintly nods assent to all her questions.)* So broken and so gray! You the Enoch Annie mourned for years—the man we all thought dead, and who went down in a storm at sea?

Enoch. Sit, Miriam, and listen to my story; nor will you wonder, when you hear it, at the shattered wreck you see before you. *(Music—descriptive-played through* ENOCH's *narrative.)* Our voyage out was fair—we traded, set sail for home, the storm came on which wrecked our ship, and drowned our crew. The captain, a sailor, and myself drifted on that wild sea all night, the rest were lost! We stranded upon an island. They that landed with me died, and I was left alone on an almost barren waste, a shipwrecked sailor waiting for a sail. How long the years I waited for that sail! The days seemed weeks, weeks months, months were years, and years were ages to me then! One day, in delirious sleep, I heard the bells of this port ring. They rang out merrily across the ocean to me, like they did the day I wed my Annie. I wondered then what made me hear those bells. I know now. *(Shudders.)* A ship touched there at last, I was taken on board, we sailed away, and landed at this port. I went to what was once my home, That home was empty, its inmates gone. You told me of her grieving and her waiting. I went to look upon her dear face again, to see if she were happy. It broke my heart. But I *am* happy now. I feel that I am going, for I'm drifting to a fairer port than any here on earth! *(Music ends.*

Miriam. *(Rises.)* Enoch Arden, will you see your children? *(He turns away.)* Do let me fetch them to you?

Enoch. Disturb me not! Let me hold my purpose till I die! Sit again! *(She sits.)* Heed me, while I have the power to speak. Tell *her,* *(moved)* that I died blessing her and our dear children! To Philip, that I prayed for him, too. He never meant us anything but good! And if my children, who hardly knew me living, care to see me dead, why let them come. But she must not, for my wan face would vex her after life! *(Miriam kisses his hand.)* And now there is but one of all my blood who is waiting to embrace me, and he is there *(points up)* in the world to come! This hair was his. *(Produces the lock he received in the second act.)* She cut it off and gave it to me on the day I went away. I have borne it with me all these years and thought to bear it with me to my grave. But now my mind is changed, for soon *(looks upward)* I shall see my little babe in heavenly bliss! When —I—am—gone—give—her—this,—it *may* bring comfort, and *must* be a token that I was her lost Enoch Arden! *(Pause.*

Miriam. *(Turns her head and speaks aside.)* Poor man! If it was not that I was promise bound, I'd bring his children even now to see the last of him before he died.

Enoch. *(In delirium.)* Ah, there is the old home—but empty— she is gone! Tut, tut, tut! Why don't she sail faster? Ah, there's Annie down on the beach a-waiting for my coming! I'll signal her! *(Waves his hand.)* Why, where are the little ones?

Miriam. He's out of his right mind. He thinks he's coming back from sea! Enoch Arden, let me fetch your children?

Enoch. Yes, bring the babes, and I'll have the boat ready. We'll all die together!

Miriam. Still crazy-like! But I would have his children see him once before he goes. I can't leave him.

Enter DR. WINTHROP, *door* L.F.

Miriam. Ah, here is Dr. Winthrop! Doctor, go to Philip Ray's, and bring Enoch Arden's children here at once.

Dr. W.   Enoch Arden's!   Why?

Miriam.   There lies their father, and he's dying!

(Points to ENOCH.

Dr. W.   They just now passed me at the door.   I'll call to them!

(Exit door L.F.   *All is silent.*

Enoch.   A sail, a sail!   *(Laughs wildly.)*   I am saved!

(Falls back dead.

Re-enter DR. WINTHROP, *door* L.F., *with* ENOCH's *son and daughter.*

Miriam.   He is gone!   There is your father!   Kneel, children, kneel!   *(Children kneel* C., *by couch.)*   Pray for the peace of the good ENOCH ARDEN!   *(Music—*"Home, Sweet Home!"   *Tableau.*

Disposition of Characters.

MIRIAM.
R.

ENOCH dead on couch, R.C.

CHILDREN *kneeling by couch,* C.

DR. WINTHROP.
L.C.

CURTAIN.